Last Minute Fiancé

Special Edition

The First Time Series

Carrie Ann Ryan

Last Minute Fiancé
A First Time Series Novel
By: Carrie Ann Ryan
© 2024 Carrie Ann Ryan

Cover Art by Sweet N Spicy Designs

All content warnings are listed on the book page for this book on my website.

Praise for CARRIE ANN Ryan

"Count on Carrie Ann Ryan for emotional, sexy, character driven stories that capture your heart!" – Carly Phillips, NY Times bestselling author

"Carrie Ann Ryan's romances are my newest addiction! The emotion in her books captures me from the very beginning. The hope and healing hold me close until the end. These love stories will simply sweep you away." ~ NYT Bestselling Author Deveny Perry

"Carrie Ann Ryan writes the perfect balance of sweet and heat ensuring every story feeds the soul." - Audrey Carlan, #1 New York Times Bestselling Author

"Carrie Ann Ryan never fails to draw readers in with passion, raw sensuality, and characters that pop off the page. Any book by Carrie Ann is an absolute treat." – New York Times Bestselling Author J. Kenner

"Carrie Ann Ryan knows how to pull your heartstrings and make your pulse pound! Her wonderful Redwood Pack series will draw you in and keep you reading long into the night. I can't wait to see what comes next with the new generation, the Talons. Keep them coming, Carrie Ann!" –Lara Adrian, New York Times bestselling author of CRAVE THE NIGHT

"With snarky humor, sizzling love scenes, and brilliant, imaginative worldbuilding, The Dante's Circle series reads as if Carrie Ann Ryan peeked at my personal wish list!" – NYT Bestselling Author, Larissa Ione

"Carrie Ann Ryan writes sexy shifters in a world full of passionate happily-ever-afters." – *New York Times* Bestselling Author Vivian Arend

"Carrie Ann's books are sexy with characters you can't help but love from page one. They are heat and heart blended to perfection." *New York Times* Bestselling Author Jayne Rylon

Carrie Ann Ryan's books are wickedly funny and deliciously hot, with plenty of twists to keep you guessing. They'll keep you up all night!" USA Today Bestselling Author Cari Quinn

"Once again, Carrie Ann Ryan knocks the Dante's Circle series out of the park. The queen of hot, sexy, enthralling paranormal romance, Carrie Ann is an author not to miss!" *New York Times* bestselling Author Marie Harte

To my 1oth grade English teacher.
Thank you for not laughing at me when I went overboard
on my essay.
And thank you for sparking that need to write more, even
though I buried it for another ten years.

Last Minute Fiancé

A single drunken night changed everything.

One positive test later, and I'm not only pregnant with my best friend's baby, but I'm falling for him too.

Except when my ex finds out at work, I do the worst thing I could at that moment: I lie.

I make up a fake fiancé and my boss overhears.

Now I need my best friend to play the part. He's good at it, too, since we can't keep our hands off each other.

When we're both forced to lean on each other, we'll have to face facts.

There's nothing fake about this relationship.

Even if I'll break my heart in the process.

Chapter One

Luca

I was a little drunk and a little too full of cake, but it didn't matter.

Because, as I said, I was a little drunk.

Music blared through the speakers as people writhed on the dance floor, laughing and joking with one another. I was pretty sure most of these people had been strangers earlier in the day, but when the birthday shots came out and the cake was cut, people became quite friendly.

That didn't bother me too much from where I stood

at the edge of the dance floor, sipping my drink and watching the others have fun.

I wasn't sure what drink I was on; I had lost count at around three. Which didn't seem like a lot, but I was usually a beer or wine drinker, not a cocktail drinker. However, these fruity concoctions tasted yummy.

And they went well with the cake that I had inhaled.

"Do you want some water?"

I blinked and narrowed my gaze at my brother, August. At least, I thought it was August, though it could have been Heath. My brothers were identical twins after all, and sometimes—if I'd had this many drinks, which wasn't often—it was hard to remember how to tell them apart. Being identical and all.

You would think that sometimes I would feel like the odd man out, being the baby brother of twins that seemed to have that twin bond thing, but I didn't. No, the odd man out was actually our sister. But Greer wasn't here, as she had left earlier with her husbands.

My brothers never made me feel like I was on the outside, the one that didn't look like them.

I squinted one eye and figured out that yes, this was August.

"Looking good, Aggie."

My brother scowled and forced a plastic cup of water in my hand. "Drink this, asshole. And next time you call me Aggie, I'll forget that you bruise like a peach and I'll kick your ass."

I snorted and looked down at both drinks in my hand. "Look at me. Double fisting." I snorted, far too pleased with myself. It had been a very hard week at the clinic, and I'd had some terrible days that I didn't want to dwell on. Tonight was about letting loose. Finally.

August pinched the bridge of his nose. "You are not in college anymore. Act normal."

"I wasn't even allowed to drink in college, thank you very much. I was in *vet school* and not old enough to drink. I'm playing catch up. You know, with parties and oats. You're supposed to sow them, right?"

"Drink your water. How many of those fruity things with whipped cream have you had?"

I looked down at the pink frothy drink and shrugged, just noticing that I spilled some water on my shoe. "Not sure. But they sure are tasty."

August scowled and took the drink from me and forced my other hand with the water cup towards my mouth.

"Drink this. You're allowed to get shit-faced; I'm not Mom or Dad."

I snorted and nearly choked on the water. "Good for that. Mom and Dad are assholes. I wouldn't like it if you were an asshole."

He gave me a sad look and cupped my cheek. "I love you, baby brother. And I'm glad I'm not Mom and Dad either. Because they are assholes. Now go drink your water and sober up a bit. You're going to hate yourself in the morning."

"I'm not sure if I hate myself now or not. The fruity drinks help."

"That sugar is going to hurt. I don't know what Heath was thinking with those fruity drinks."

"It's my bar, and my wife wanted a fun drink."

"Okay," I said, grinning. "I like that she's your wife. Devney's great."

Heath looked between us, and the look on his face was so full of exasperation, I couldn't help but grin before taking another drink of my water.

"My God. How many of those has he had? They're just sugar and alcohol. He's going to hate himself in the morning and I'm going to be blamed for it."

"I lost count," I said proudly, putting my hand over my stomach.

"Do not throw up in my bar," Heath growled.

"Maybe don't let him have so many fruity drinks,"

August said, smiling between us. "He's your problem now."

"Hell no. I'm watching over my wife who also drank too much, and I'm going to go tuck her into bed soon. Party's almost over guys. Drink more water."

I did as both of them said, on my third glass of water. Heath slid a basket of fries in front of me and I smiled dreamily at him. "Seriously, my favorite brother."

"You literally just said that to me," August added dryly before he maneuvered someone else to sit next to me.

I squinted at the newcomer before beaming. "My Addison!" I called out, probably a little too loudly.

"My Luca!" My new best friend wrapped her arms around my shoulders and hugged me tight. "I lost you."

"You guys were like five feet from each other," August grumbled. "I need to go check on everyone else and make sure they have rides home. Do not move from this spot."

"Of course not. I have my new best friend here. I love Luca. You're still an asshole." She winked at August.

My brother rolled his eyes as he made sure Addison sat down. "Stop talking to my ex-wife."

"But your ex-wife is my friend. I had to go with girl solidarity."

"You are going to regret this conversation in the morning," August grumbled before he went off to go presumably help someone else.

I pulled away from Addison and scooted the fries between us. I took a bite of the gloriously crunchy deep-fried potatoes, and sighed. "You shouldn't get on him about the divorce. It makes him sad."

Addison exhaled, her mouth going in that little pout I told myself I shouldn't think about as much as I did. "You're right. It's such a jerk move of me. I don't even know why I said it. It's not like Paisley treats him any differently. Not that I've ever really seen them together outside the wedding and random events like this."

"I don't even know why they got divorced. Only that one minute they seemed happy, the next he came home and said it hadn't worked out. And then she was living in this state with us."

"But it wasn't on purpose. I'm pretty sure Paisley was here first." Addison frowned. "Yes. She was totally here first. And then you guys showed up." She smiled at me before she crunched into a fry.

"Not that I mind. Because Heath and Devney are adorable, and we got Greer—your sister is fantastic."

"She is pretty fantastic." I paused, waiting for her to continue. "And me. You got to meet me. And that really is the best part of your year."

She rolled her eyes. "Of course, *you*. My life wouldn't be complete without you." She fluttered her eyelashes.

I snorted. "I feel like you're mocking me."

"Of course I'm mocking you. Because I love you."

I sighed and finished the fries with her, as well as our waters. "You know, I kind of miss women telling me that they love me. Or at least one woman." I frowned. "I'm really glad I have water, since I'm drunk enough to be bringing that up." I rubbed at my chest then drank the last of my water. August appeared with two more cups, scowling between the two of us. He shook his head, as if he wanted to say something and refrained, before going back to talk with a group of friends.

"You can always talk about her if you want. I don't mind."

"There's nothing to talk about." I shrugged. "She's gone. I'm not. I'm here. I'm sobering up." I swallowed, the taste of sugar and liquor still lingering on my tongue. "Okay, not sober, but I'm not silly anymore. I'm going to count that as a win."

"I like silly Luca."

"I like you too, Addison."

Our gazes met and my stomach tightened. I must have had far more to drink than I thought. This was Addison. Yes, she was beautiful, one of the most beautiful women I had ever met in my life. *And* she was my best friend.

I loved her bright light-blue eyes and her short dark hair. It was just past her shoulders now, having grown out from a pixie cut before I had met her. She mentioned once that her hair had been down past her back, and because her ex had always loved talking about it, she chopped it off when they broke up.

I thought she looked good no matter what, but she didn't believe me when I told her that. Her hair was great, and so were her eyes, but it was that smile that always caught me. She had such a damn good smile, one that brought you in and let you know that she could take over the world, and you could be right by her side. That nothing bad could happen when that smile was near.

Not that I would ever tell her, that seemed a little too weird to say out loud.

"Okay you two, let's get you in a rideshare and get you home."

I blinked up in confusion at August. "But Addison and I don't live together."

"You live close enough, and the guy already has it set up that you guys can share the ride and get you both there. I can't take you home when I'm dealing with everyone else. Did the fries and water help?" He studied our faces, and before we could answer, he nodded and pulled me up by my shoulder.

"Come on. Get home, drink more water, take a couple Advil, and go to bed. Thank God you don't have to work tomorrow, but you're still going to hate me, hate all of us, if you don't get some sleep." He scowled again at Addison. "You too. In fact, I've never seen you drink. Is something going on?"

I whirled on her, staggering a bit as I did. Thankfully, my brother kept me steady, though he didn't look happy about it.

"That's right. You don't get drunk. Is it work? Am I going to have to kick someone's ass for you, because I will. You never let me kick anyone's ass."

Addison smiled and leaned forward, patting my cheek.

"You're the sweetest. But no. No asses need to be hurt. I mean, unless that's something you like."

I grinned as August choked from beside me, shaking his head.

"I do not understand the two of you, nor whatever type of psycho parasitic relationship you have, but it doesn't matter. I'm getting you in the car, and the driver's going to text me when he drops you off. Go home, drink water, and get some sleep."

"But I didn't tell the birthday girl goodbye."

I looked around August to search for Devney, and August growled, pulling us towards the door.

"Devney is already on her way home, asleep in the back of the car, because she had just as much as you for her birthday."

"That's good. Devney never gets to really have fun anymore."

"She has tons of fun. And because all one hundred and fifty of her siblings showed up, the place was hopping."

"There weren't one hundred and fifty, only like eighty-four," I corrected, and August rolled his eyes before shoving me in the back of a car. I slammed my head into the oh-shit bar and groaned, clasping my palm to the side of my head as Addison slid into the other side. The driver said something to August, but I wasn't paying attention, too busy breathing through the pain inside my head.

"Oh, poor baby. Let me kiss it better."

She pulled me towards her and kissed my temple. Her lips were so damn soft, I sucked in a breath, annoyed that my cock was standing at attention. With so much to drink that shouldn't be the case but apparently my dick didn't care. It had been too long since it got any attention, but it didn't matter. I wasn't going to do anything about it. This was Addison. My dick could get over her, just like I'd been trying to do since we'd met.

Addison pulled me so I was resting on her shoulder, but it wasn't her shoulder, it was more like her breasts because we hit a bump and I slid down. She didn't move me though, so I snuggled in, her breasts soft and voluptuous. The perfect fucking pillows for my hurt head.

It was a fifteen-minute drive, or at least that's what it should be, it could have been an hour for all I knew—I was in paradise—when the driver pulled up in front of the house.

"Here you go."

"Perfect," Addison said as she moved, and I reluctantly slid away from her breasts.

She got out of the car and I followed, not just because of her boobs.

The driver said something, but we waved him off and he sighed before driving away.

"Weird," Addison muttered, and I followed her into the house. She closed the door behind us and we made our way into the kitchen.

"Water and Advil, just like your brother said."

I grinned and we each chugged a whole glass of water, my head finally no longer aching.

"I'm not as drunk as before. That's a good thing."

She smiled wide. "Me either."

Then she stepped past me, stripping her shirt over her head.

When the bra came next, I swallowed hard, trying not to look at her rosy pink nipples. But it was really the only thing I could look at.

And when she moved back to tug on my belt, I sucked in a breath and followed her into the bedroom.

I stripped down, taking off my shirt first, then my belt and pants, forgetting I was still wearing my shoes, and quickly kicked those off.

"I had such a great time tonight," Addison said as she stretched her arms over her head.

That put her breasts right near my face as I was bent over taking my shoes off, and so I did the only thing I could think.

I slid my face between her breasts and kissed her. She moaned, and somehow we were suddenly both on the bed, hands and mouths all over each other.

I didn't mean for it to happen.

My mouth was on hers, and she tasted of sugar and liquor and everything that I craved.

I slid my hand between her legs and found her bare. She was wet, my fingers sliding between her wet folds. I slid one finger deep inside and she moaned.

It felt like a dream, like it wasn't real, but the screaming part in the back of my brain knew it was real.

"Addison?" I whispered. "Tell me to stop."

She looked at me, her eyes clear.

"I'm not that drunk, Luca. Don't stop."

So I didn't.

With my hand still between her legs, I slid my thumb over her clit, slowly fingerfucking her as she writhed under me. Her hands went between us, gripping the base of my cock, and I groaned, needing more.

We were still kissing, her hands on me, when she came, her pussy clenching around my fingers.

When I slowly slid them out of her, I brought my hand up to my mouth and sucked them clean.

She groaned, then turned over.

I looked down and began massaging her ass, spreading her cheeks so I could see her wetness.

"You're so damn beautiful."

She let out a soft laugh as she placed the condom between us.

Suddenly far more sober, I quickly opened the packet and slid the condom over my length.

And then she was under me again and I was cradled between her thighs.

I met her gaze and knew that this was probably a fucking mistake.

But I didn't care. Not with this woman, not with what I knew was going to happen next.

I slid deep inside of her and we both moaned, and then my lips were on hers, and her hands were rubbing up and down my back.

It was fast, it was frantic, but she was coming again around my cock, squeezing me, as I slid in and out of her faster and harder. And when I pounded in the last time, both of us whispering each other's names, I came, my whole body shaking as she clung to me.

Sweat-slick, and now sober, I held her but couldn't meet her gaze.

So afraid that I had ruined everything.

"Luca?" she whispered, and I was prepared for the blow, prepared for any reaction.

I pulled back and pushed her hair back from her face, needing to see those eyes. "Addison?"

"We'll talk about it in the morning?" she asked, her voice soft, afraid of what I would say.

So in answer, I kissed my best friend again, slowly, surely, and then I pulled out of her, kissing her again before taking care of the condom.

But when I slid back into bed, she snuggled into my arms.

"In the morning," I whispered.

Only I didn't think we would.

I didn't think there was anything to say.

I had just had sex with my best friend.

There was no coming back from that.

Chapter Two

Addison

For some reason I had the meme stuck in my head of the little teacup piglet twerking thanks to a loop of streaming. And that pig kept twerking to the sound of Rihanna's "Work." Because all it felt like I was doing these days was working.

But I was not nearly as adorable as the sweet little teacup pig, nor did I have the gloriousness that was Rihanna's ass. Nobody needed to see me twerking.

All I was doing was working.

Of course, that wasn't all I was doing, considering I

had the memories of something that I shouldn't have done swirling through my mind.

I loved my job, I really did. But sometimes it felt like my job was trying to kill me.

I loved being in finance and I was a damn good investment banker. And yet, dealing with finance bros meant that I worked twice as hard for half the gains.

So I always had to be focused. I had to have my mind in the game, numbers at my fingertips, and I needed to work on projected growth and investments. I had a dual degree in finance and economics, and an MBA in finance from a top school. I had left my friends and family back in Denver to go to that top school out of state and came back to work at one of the top finance companies in the country. It was the top one in Denver, and I kicked ass at it when they actually saw me doing it.

So I needed to keep my mind focused.

And not on something from two months ago.

I did not need to think of Luca. Or the fact that I could remember what he tasted like. Or remembered what he felt like when he was thrusting in and out of me, how he was so careful. Even though we were anything but careful with what we had done with each other that night.

In the years since we met, we had become best friends and were too involved in each other's lives.

It hadn't even been two years since we met and everything clicked. I had known that I wanted this man in my life, but not for romantic reason. Why would I want to go down that romantic alley? Romance killed. It ruined lives.

Romance got in the way of what was important.

Succeeding, achieving, and being strategic about your life.

My five- to ten-year plan did not include a man.

The last time I included a man in my life plans, everything had gone to shit and I was still reaping the consequences of that—wallowing in the ramifications of falling in love with a dumbass who happened to be in the same career as me, and happened to be at the same level as me at our current company.

Because of course, we both loved fucking Denver, Colorado, and loved the mountain view and air and the fact that we had sun even when it was zero degrees outside.

So we had both moved back here after grad school and started at the same damn company. I knew what it meant to work with your ex, to hate the man you had once let inside you.

I was not about to be the jaded bitter bitch ex-girlfriend. So I worked with him, I dealt with the snide jokes, I dealt with the finance dude-bro mentality every day with every single man that worked with me. And there was a lot of men considering this had somehow become the old guard boys club even though we were supposed to be an enlightened society. Well, fuck that; we all knew that was a lie.

I knew that falling in love and going down that path and being with someone—other than a single night where names didn't matter and neither did orgasms—would only lead to heartache and insanity.

I knew that none of that mattered.

I knew that taking a chance and being with someone that actually mattered would only break you and stand in the way in the end.

Luca was not part of my five- to ten-year plan.

He was my friend. He was my confidant. He was the guy I got drunk with and knew I would always be safe with.

Except I had been the one to kiss him. Which led to what else happened that night.

If either one of us had been in our right mind, it wouldn't have happened.

Of course, I knew I was lying to myself. Completely lying to myself.

Because even buzzed, no longer drunk, he had asked for consent and I had freely given it to him. I lied to myself and said we would talk about it the next morning.

But of course, we hadn't. No, I had pretended to be asleep as he rolled away the next morning and called himself a rideshare to go home. That walk of shame had been in the early morning hours where nobody was truly awake enough to notice.

And we had seen each other every week since. After all, my other best friend was married to his brother. So of course I would see him.

We hadn't talked about it except for the fact that knowing we hadn't talked about it meant we were firmly of the same mind.

We would remain friends. We would pretend it hadn't happened, and we would go about our business as if everything was normal and nothing had been fundamentally changed.

Because of course it hadn't.

We were adults. Maybe this was a new age, where you could have sex with someone, amazing sex where you could still remember the toe-curling orgasms that had made you see stars. Maybe all of that could happen and then you could move on and just be friends.

Because it wasn't like I was ever going to have sex again. There wasn't enough time for that, based on the paperwork in front of me and the never-ending emails.

I needed to stop thinking about Luca. I needed to focus.

Luca mattered because he was my friend, but he didn't matter when it came to my sex life.

That would never happen again.

Of course, if it hadn't truly mattered, if it meant nothing other than a quick release between two friends who cared about each other, why hadn't I told Devney or Paisley about it?

I knew the answer to that. Because that would make it important. And then they would want to talk about it. And then I would freak out and want to actually figure out what the hell I was feeling.

I didn't want to do that.

"Lily, you got the Franklin report?" a deep voice asked from the doorway, and I looked up quickly, ignoring the slight sense of dizziness from the motion.

I hadn't eaten enough that day, because I'd been queasy off and on thanks to the major report that was coming up. I had finished it, but then they added a new addendum so I needed to go back through it all and it had taken all night. All night where I hadn't been feeling great thanks to the stress of this fucking job.

But this was fine, this was just one rung on the ladder that I needed to climb to get to where I wanted. And I would get there. I was hardworking and damn good at this. I could make money, and I could make people happy.

"Yes. All done and it's in your inbox now."

My boss frowned. "Really? I didn't see it."

I looked at the string again. "It's in my sent. It's also attached."

"Can you print it out for me? And perhaps help me with that PDF again? I don't know why they keep changing the file names."

I smiled brightly and pretended that this didn't happen every single time I sent him anything.

I wasn't sure it happened with anyone else. Probably because those men were guys and of course my boss would never ask them how to open a PDF. Even though all he had to do was double-click it. Or even hit return. Or even blink at it and it would probably open faster than me walking to his office and doing it for him.

"It's in your inbox now, sir."

"I need you to open it for me, Lily. And print it out. In duplicate. Armstrong and I will meet you in the office."

I disliked the fact that my boss called us by our last names, as if we were on some sports ball team. I was not on a sports ball team. I'd played field hockey in high school but hadn't had time or willpower to play in college. So I was used to the last name thing somewhat, but it was a little different when you were on the field with people who understood you and didn't treat you like the little woman. Now though, I got to be called by my last name, which also happened to be a first name of a woman. Somehow it felt demoralizing, like I was their precious lily, easily crumpled, and used for funerals and wakes.

And okay, that was enough thinking on that line because I was clearly losing my damn mind.

"Yeah, Lily. Better print those out."

I raised a brow at Travis Armstrong, my ex-boyfriend and nemesis. I hated him. Not that he really mattered because I rarely worked with him. Yes we had worked on this project together—I had done most of the work while he second-guessed everything I did. But here he was, walking practically arm in arm with the boss while I had to print out things.

I was not their administrative assistant. He still called them God damn secretaries, even though the women in those positions had asked HR to stop using that term. But in order for HR to do anything about it, they needed to have spines.

There were always little ways to get around everything, and these "good old boys" had always been very good at it. It didn't matter what the rules said, they always found exceptions. And that's why I did what I could to stay on the ball and keep ahead of things. Though I was still a little nauseous and I felt like I was two steps behind. That was going to get me in trouble, so I needed to fix this. It was now or never.

I pulled out the three folders with each of our names on them. This wasn't my first rodeo, and I had been anticipating something like this. I mean, why would the man know how to open up a PDF on his own computer? Behind our boss, Travis' eyes narrowed slightly and I gave him a bright smile. *Take that asshole.* Yes I had been forced to do the work anyway, but those two wouldn't be walking together side by side talking about anything from golfing or the account itself while I got left behind.

That would not be happening. Especially not with my ex.

I handed over the paperwork and stepped between them, my pace brisk.

"On to the office?"

"Thanks for printing those out, doll."

I raised a brow at Travis and he just grinned.

Why would I go to HR? Why would I upset anyone? Especially because HR was dating one of the bosses. Ethics—what was the point of them? I couldn't really go outside the process, not when things would blow up in my face, and it was easier to just get the work done.

The fact that I kept having to remind myself that I loved my job and I loved doing what I did, meant maybe that wasn't entirely true and something needed to change. But not anytime soon. There had already been enough changes.

By the time we got to the office, I was seething as well as nauseous. I should have eaten that morning, but I'd been so focused on making sure that I kept a leg up on Travis that I hadn't. And now I was regretting the cup of coffee and two bites of bagel that I had rather than an actual meal.

As we went over the account, and Travis needled me at every single turn, I needled him right back. I knew what I was doing, and this man and all his little digs were not going to get at me. They hadn't in college, and they wouldn't now. I didn't know anymore why I dated him, other than I hadn't seen him for what he was truly was. But now I did, and I was better than that.

As we stood up for our lunch break, my stomach revolted and I nearly tripped on my heels, putting my hand over my belly.

Travis raised a brow while my boss frowned.

"Lily?"

I held up my hand, knowing if I didn't move quickly, this was going to end badly. I practically sprinted to the women's restroom, past the guys making lewd comments that I wasn't supposed to hear, slammed the door behind me, and locked myself in a stall. I nearly went to my knees, but then thought better of it, before bending over and hurling out everything that had been left in my stomach.

My knees shook and my stomach continued to whirl as I threw up again, and then used the toilet tissue to wipe my face.

I was clammy, but felt slightly better from having thrown up. I flushed the toilet, then went to the sink to wipe my face.

I frowned as I washed out my mouth and wiped my face. I needed to go to my desk and clean up my makeup a bit, and I would. Eventually.

Damn it. I couldn't believe I'd just gotten sick in front of my boss and my ex. Could this day be any worse?

But no, I wasn't going to make a scene beyond this. I would go back to work and everything would be fine.

I held my chin high, ignored the fact that I was already queasy again, and made my way outside into the office.

Everybody was back to work, but I couldn't help overhearing a deep voice that was Travis' best work friend.

"Must be her time of the month," the guy mumbled

and Travis laughed. I was making my way to my office, my hand over my stomach, and I nearly froze when what he said sank in, my hands shaking. Because no. That couldn't be the case.

Only it might be.

No. That couldn't be right. This was just food poisoning. Or a stomach bug.

No. Damn it.

I shut the door behind me and pulled out my phone to call Luca. Because I needed my best friend.

Not just to talk to him.

But to maybe ruin everything.

Again.

<hr>

I was not a fan of waiting. It broke time into measurements that either slowed down or sped up, depending on what you were waiting for.

I wanted to know, needed to know what would happen once I finished this.

But that meant I would have to wait for it.

"Addison?"

I turned to see Luca standing there, my best friend. Well, one of them. Somehow, when the world hadn't been watching, Luca Cassidy had become my best friend.

Devney was my childhood best friend, and would always be like a sister. Paisley was quickly becoming a best friend.

But there was one thing I learned growing up, that those words mattered and changed over time. That I could have more than one best friend. Each person in my life meant something different to me.

Luca and I had clicked the moment we met. I would be forever grateful that Devney had faked a relationship with his brother.

"What?" I asked when he said something. I was lost in my own thoughts, trying to figure out what was going on.

Because honestly this all felt like a dream.

"I asked if you needed something to drink. You know. To help."

I snorted, because he looked just as lost as I did.

"I'm really not good at this, Luca."

"You too? Because this is a first for me. And I'm not good at firsts."

"Oh, I'm pretty sure you're good at firsts," I joked before I sat down on the bar stool next and put my hands over my face and screamed.

Luca was there in an instant, his hands on my shoulders as he kept me steady.

That was Luca, the steady one.

I pretended to be steady. But in reality I freaked out and screamed and only pretended I knew what I was doing.

But I didn't. I had no idea what to do or how to fix it.

"Do you want to go for a walk? Do you want food? Please, just tell me what to do right now."

I lowered my hands and looked up at my best friend. "I have no idea what to do either. This is really poor timing."

"Well, I think it's the timing that needed to happen."

I blinked. "Are you trying to spout off sage crap that makes no sense but sounds good so you feel better and in control of the situation?"

Luca nodded. "Of course. It's how I work with cats who really don't want anything to do with me. I talk calmly, and then my staff and I tackle the poor thing and hide its little head so it's not scared anymore."

I blinked, trying to figure out where he was going with this. "Are you saying I'm an uncontrollable cat with a biting issue?"

Luca smirked, his eyes going dark and smokey. "Oh, I know you like biting."

I froze for a minute before I snorted and laughed,

flipping him off. It was exactly the reaction he wanted because I knew he was trying to relax both of us.

"So, seen any good movies lately?" he asked.

"You know I've been working eighty-hour weeks and I don't know what movies are anymore."

Luca sat next to me, his hand on mine as we waited. And waited. "You work longer hours than I do, and I don't get any time off."

He gestured toward the sleeping elderly collie mix currently on my couch. When Luca had shown up right after I texted him saying it was an emergency, he had the elderly dog with him. I normally wasn't a pet-on-furniture type of person, but I had seen those wide eyes, and not just Luca's, and known that Reginald the Fifth needed to have anything he wanted.

"I hate that his owners aren't here anymore and now Reginald doesn't have any family but us."

"I'm not good at family, Luca. I'm good at working, and fighting for what I need. I'm really not good at this."

"You can be. And we both know Reginald's sick. We'll take care of him for his last days so he won't be alone."

I blinked tears away. "It's not fair they don't get as much time as we do."

"As is evidenced by Reginald's parents, time is short for everyone. Reginald's happy right now. He has people who love him and will make sure he's comfy. And he's sleeping on your precious, precious couch that you don't even let me sit on."

"That was one time, and you were sweaty from a run. You could have sat in that chair, but no, you wanted to sprawl all over my new couch."

"And tonight you put sheets on your couch so Reginald would be comfortable. You're a good woman, Addison. That's why you're my friend."

He squeezed my hand right as my phone buzzed.

We both looked down at the alarm, tension riding us.

No, this wasn't true. Totally not happening.

But time didn't lie, it sneered at you, and kicked you in the ass. But it didn't lie.

I walked into the bathroom, Luca right on my heels, and we looked down.

And saw my world change.

Everything changed.

"Well, fuck," Luca murmured, bringing me out of the screaming inside my head that wouldn't stop.

The little window in front clearly said it all.

Pregnant.

I was pregnant.

Single.

Working eighty hours a week in a job that I loved

with people that I hated. A job where being a woman was more than a mark against you, it was something you had to overcome.

And now I was gestating.

I was single. Alone, standing next to my best friend.

And pregnant.

This day couldn't possibly get any worse.

And with that thought, I whirled to the toilet and emptied my stomach—my best friend holding back my hair, and the father of my unborn baby as pale as I was.

Chapter Three

Luca

There was an odd sense of panic running through my system. One that screamed that I should be reacting, that I should be fighting or fleeing. Could someone flee and fight at the same time? Because that felt like the correct response.

I looked down at the test in her hand, and heard the words coming out of her mouth, but they didn't quite register.

We hadn't gone for one of those tests that were hard to read. Not one where you had to see if the little rattle was pink or blue or purple or polka dot. Not one you had to count the lines or decide if the lines were dotted or straight or diagonal. No, we got the one that said pregnant or not pregnant. And if you looked at the screen you realized that the word "pregnant" would always be there and it was just the word "not" that might show up on the readout. Meaning there was still potential for the "not" to show up. I stared at it, willing the word "not" to slowly fade into reality.

But it never did. The "not" did not show up. Instead, all that remained was a single word —pregnant.

As in the woman that had quickly become my best friend, my confidant, the woman that I enjoyed hanging out with, that I had slept with one time while a little too drunk and a little too happy, who was now carrying my child.

She hadn't said she hadn't slept with anyone else, and had invited me here because she needed me by her side. Not as her friend, no, as the dickhead who had impregnated her.

I ran my hands over my face, trying not to panic and yet all I was doing was freaking the fuck out.

"Oh my God."

"That's what I'm saying," Addison screeched, then set the test gently down on the counter and picked up the other box. "We're going to do this one more time. Or maybe eight more times, until it comes up with the right answer."

"I'm going to go get you some water, or Gatorade. You need to pee."

"Yes." She snapped her fingers twice and pointed at me. "Get me hydrated and then I'm going to pee over everything."

"I'm so glad that we're not freaking out and we're acting rational," I said, as we both burst out laughing, but I knew each of us were on the verge of tears.

I ran to the kitchen and got two bottles of water and a Gatorade.

I swayed a bit, realizing that the nausea I was feeling had nothing to do with the nausea she was feeling. Because she had needed the Gatorade because she had been having morning sickness.

Because Addison was pregnant.

I dry heaved for a minute, bent over at the waist, my full hands on my knees. My God. Addison was pregnant. No. These tests were going to come up with the correct answer soon. Because false positives totally happened all the time, didn't they?

Okay. I was a vet. A veterinarian who dealt with pregnant animals, not people, though I knew the stats behind false positives when it came to at-home pregnancy tests.

The stats were not in my favor, but fuck it. I had been a child genius according to my family. I had graduated early, ended up in college far too early, made some terrible decisions and some great ones. I owned a veterinary clinic with another person who was great at the business side of things, not so much at the people side of things, and I had done all of this before I was thirty. I was smart. I knew statistics. And I knew we were fucked because we had fucked.

That was going to be my new tagline. I was going to put it on shirts and let everyone know that I was a fucking idiot who just impregnated my best friend.

I was so glad that I wasn't panicking. I was handling this like a complete professional and not having an actual meltdown.

Everything was going to be fine, but I needed to calm down. Because Addison needed me to be strong. She needed me to be calm and collected.

The bathroom door was closed, so I waited until she opened it again, another test in her hand. I handed over the electrolyte drink, and she shook her head before taking the water bottle.

"My stomach hurts a little too much for flavoring." We looked at each other but didn't talk about it. Because maybe it was just a stomach flu. A lot of stomach flu. That would not bring a baby into the world.

I took the sports drink and chugged a good third of it while not making eye contact. Neither one of us said anything as we waited for the clock to wind down. The next two tests said pregnant, and we stood there, hands shaking.

"Addison."

"I can't be on birth control."

I blinked at the topic change, but nodded. "Okay. That's fine. I mean, I guess that makes sense?" I was rambling at this point.

"Luca, I can't have hormonal birth control because I have blood clot issues. That's why even when completely drunk I made sure that we used a condom. We made sure. It doesn't make any sense. I...I can't believe this is true...that life could do this...but...I'm pregnant, Luca."

I was still trying to catch up with what she had said.

We stood in her small guest bathroom in her cozy house that she loved and had put so much work into when she wasn't working sixty- and eighty-hour weeks. I painted this bathroom because it had been an odd olive color, and she wanted to brighten it up a bit, so we had added dark blue batten board with a very light white paint on the top. It had almost felt nautical, so she added a few more tree and barren wood paintings. All in all, it felt welcoming, and I was happy to have helped make it what it was.

That I could be a part of it.

She pushed past me after setting the test down on the counter and began to pace the living room. I followed her, my hands in my pockets because I didn't know what to do with them. If I did what I wanted to do with them, I'd have her in my arms and we'd be pretending this hadn't happened.

"I cannot believe this is happening. I'm always so careful. We were so careful. I'm not on birth control because my body can't handle it."

"And we used a condom."

"And we used a condom, but we know it's not a hundred percent."

"And we were so drunk, I'm honestly surprised that I could even get it up," I said, trying to lighten the situation a little.

She snorted before her eyes went wide. "Why couldn't you have had whiskey dick?"

I snorted. "Because I had tequila. And I didn't have tequila dick. So, we slept together, and then we purposely didn't talk about it other than knowing that we were just going to remain friends, right?"

"I know. I know. Oh God, I'm pregnant. And I have no idea what to do about it. I'm not ready to be a mom."

"Okay." I didn't have anything to say to that. I was still catching up to about eight sentences ago.

"I'm not ready to be a mom. I work too much, I don't eat right, I barely work out. The only times I get to see you guys are when everyone forces me to group events, or when you show up to help me with something on this house. A house that I could barely afford. And it doesn't even feel like my home yet because I'm rarely here. And now I'm supposed to be a mom?"

"We're not going to panic. We're going to be okay."

"I am clearly panicking here. Please panic with me. I need you to panic with me."

I moved forward and gripped her shoulders, taking a deep breath. "Addison. We're friends. We're always going to be friends, no matter what happens. We're going to figure this out."

"Your voice is going a little more high-pitched as you're talking, so I don't know if you're supposed to be calming me down or if I'm supposed to be calming you down."

"Okay. This is what we're going to do. We're going to panic, but we're also going to make an appointment with the doctor. Because no matter what, you're not going through this alone. Even if you got pregnant by some random guy and not me."

"Are you fucking kidding me right now?"

"I'm trying to put out a hypothetical here, not actually say anything. What I'm saying is even if I hadn't been the one with the super sperm, I would still be by your side. So, now me and my super sperm are going to be by your side."

"Please stop calling it super sperm."

"I promise never to use those words again." I sighed. "We're going to figure this out. We're going to go to the doctor and they're going to tell us you're not pregnant."

"We both know that is a lie."

"Fine. We're going to go to the doctor, and they're going to tell us what happens next. And they're going to make sure you're okay." I swallowed the panic in my throat as she met my gaze. I had a feeling she knew exactly why I was panicking.

All I could think about is what would happen if she wasn't okay. Because I had lost Ashleigh. How could I even contemplate the fact that I could lose someone I cared for again? No, I wasn't going to go down that path. I couldn't go down that path and remain sane. I knew this, she knew this, and we were going to be fine.

Only nothing felt fine right now.

"Luca." She ran her hands over her face and began to pace around the living room again. "I want to be a mom."

I swallowed hard and nodded. "Okay. Okay."

"I thought it would come later though. When I had my life together. When I was married. Okay, maybe not married because I always thought that was slightly archaic."

"I think it's more of a puritanical thing, right?" I said. I had once thought I would get married and it hadn't worked out. Because life hit you hard, and I lost Ashleigh before we had a chance. We had been too young, had loved too hard, and in the end she died—and was the only other person I had been with besides Addison. But I wasn't going to bring that up. That would just complicate matters, and I didn't want to think about Ashleigh.

I hated thinking about her. About the fact that I had loved her with all of my heart, and then she was gone. Gone in an instant, and I had lost my future. Because I thought we would get married and have 2.5 kids and own a house and have a Volvo. All of those things, while bringing home random animals from the vet that needed help overnight. And I would annoy Ashleigh with the number of puppies and kittens in the house. And suddenly Ashleigh was gone and there was no getting that future back. There was no fixing it.

But then Addison's words came back to me and things started to meld together and I knew I needed to split them apart before I had another panic attack.

I couldn't put Addison and Ashleigh in the same positions. I couldn't reconcile the fact that if Addison had such health issues, I could lose her. I wasn't going to think about that. That would be ridiculous. We didn't even know if she was truly pregnant. So we weren't going to stress.

"Okay, maybe not married, but I would be in a happy and healthy relationship. And I would have a partner."

"I'm standing right here. You're my best friend, Addison."

"You're my best friend. Along with Devney and Paisley, but I didn't sleep with them. I slept with you. Because we were drunk, and we used a condom, but my body hates me. It's like this fertile land that just won't stop ruining my life." She began to pace again.

"I always thought I'd be a dad, Addison. That I'd have that provincial life we joke about."

She looked at me with sadness in her gaze, and I knew she understood. That we both did.

"And you didn't get that. I'm so sorry, and I don't know what to do because I'm not her. I'm me, and I'm freaking the fuck out. I just want this all to go away but it won't. I have a report due in the morning. I don't have time for a doctor's appointment. I don't have time to deal with morning sickness and swollen ankles and everything that comes with pregnancy. I don't even know *what* comes with pregnancy. I don't know what to do now. We weren't supposed to get pregnant, Luca. I realized that there's always consequences for our actions, but I thought we were being smart."

I moved forward as she continued to ramble, and pulled her close. She fought for a moment, shaking a bit, before letting out a deep sigh and resting her head on my chest. I set my chin on the top of her head and wrapped my arms around her tightly. It took a moment before she finally wrapped her arms around me, and we just stood there, not speaking.

"I don't want to tell anyone until we have answers. Because they're going to have judgments, they're going to have questions, and I don't have any answers."

"Okay, as your best friend, I'm going to be the one to say that we are going to do this together. I don't know what this is, I don't know what happens next, but you're not alone."

"Luca."

"No. Nothing feels real right now, it all feels like panic, but that doesn't matter. We're going to do this one step at a time, and we're going to probably panic and make all the mistakes, but we're friends. Friends can do anything. You're not alone in this. We've got this."

She moved back to look at me, and I knew she didn't believe me.

Because the problem was, I didn't believe me either.

We were royally and truly screwed.

Everything had changed, and there were no answers, no labels for what was next.

I was having a baby with my best friend, and I barely remembered the night we had been together.

That was going to be a great start to a story that we'd have to tell our friends.

One day.

Unless we moved away and never talked to them again. That would probably be safer. Less judgment. Less noise.

And a whole lot more panic.

Chapter Four

Addison

Living in a state of denial seemed to be subtly working. That, or I had lost my mind enough that it didn't matter.

My stomach was still slightly achy, but I had gone over twenty-four hours without emptying it. I had to count that for a win, considering the past week I had been throwing up more often than I was keeping things down.

I still couldn't believe that I was pregnant.

A doctor's test had confirmed it, and I couldn't change that fact. Not that I was sure I wanted to.

I told Luca the truth. I had always wanted to be a mom. It was on my five- to ten-year plan. Getting pregnant with my best friend's baby? Not the plan. But it wasn't as if we had done this on purpose. It had just happened. It was fate.

And my life was stressing me out to the point that I wasn't making much sense.

I had gone right back to work too, ignoring the fact that my life was going to change forever. That was fine, because it felt as if my life was constantly changing. After coming back home from grad school, I knew that finding my place within the company was going to be challenging. Not because I wasn't talented, but because it was a very complicated and cutthroat business. Not all companies were like that, but this one had a reputation for it, and it also had the reputation for being the best.

And I wanted to be the best.

My parents had raised me like that. I was their only child, and my parents were amazing. They worked hard, they took care of each other, and loved me. They helped me through school, and we made sure that I wouldn't be in student loan debt for the rest of my life. I was in finance for a reason. I was good at what I did, but sometimes it felt like it was all I did.

Things were going to change, I knew that, but I was going to live in this state of denial for a little bit longer.

I was at my desk frowning over paperwork when someone knocked on the doorframe. I looked up to see one of the junior partners and smiled.

Nathan was a good guy, he didn't kick anyone's feet out from under them and he didn't talk shit about people behind their backs. They couldn't get him fired or take his clients. He was at the top of the food chain and had gotten there ethically and with honor.

He was exactly what I was trying to emulate. The moral high ground while still being damn good at your job.

Because I refused to be my ex.

"Hey, I was just on my way to get lunch if you want to join?"

I raised a brow. Nathan didn't ask me to lunch, and I didn't usually go out with just one of them. In fact, I was very good about making sure that I went out with the guys only in a group—I had even learned to golf though I hated it. We were getting into a pickleball era, and I was much better at that. The fact that I had kicked Travis's ass one day was the icing on the cake on an already beautiful day.

"Oh. That's nice of you to ask, but I'm working."

Nathan shook his head. "Sorry. I meant would you like to talk about our next client over lunch and get out of here while a certain group decides to have a shouting fest in the conference room next door?"

I frowned, looking down at my watch.

"Who is having a fighting fest?"

"The man currently vying for the promotion you should get."

I stood up quickly, ignoring the dizziness, and grabbed my purse.

"Are you kidding me?"

"I'm not. We both know that either of you could handle that position, but only one of you would thrive in it. You know my stance on it, now we need to get the big boss's stance."

The big boss, as in Harrington-Wells III.

I wanted that promotion. I *needed* it. It was part of my plan. And I could work from home more and set my own hours better. This would be great for the baby.

The baby I was currently denying, but that was neither here nor there.

I needed this, and I was perfect for it.

And if Travis and his goons were going to be working towards getting him the promotion, I needed someone on my side.

And a junior partner? Well, that would be good. Because that was where Nathan was. And if Nathan wanted me to have that position, then I'd work for it.

"I'd love to go to lunch." I paused. "Just lunch."

Nathan smiled softly. "I should mention that my wife and her assistant will be at the lunch too. Because while my wife and I love each other and trust each other, and I trust you, I don't trust whatever the other guys who work here will say if they happen to see us out at lunch."

Relief flooded me even as I rolled my eyes. "You got to love social dynamics and clawing your way to the top."

"You don't claw, but you do climb. So, let's make sure that happens. And, by the way, my wife would totally trust us out to a work lunch, just like we trust each other. You're welcome to bring whoever you're dating to work events, you know, that would probably help the situation."

I mumbled something under my breath, because I knew he wasn't actually fishing, he was just being helpful. When we had work events—including the one coming up soon, which was a long weekend event with two overnights—it was helpful to bring your spouse or significant other. Harrington-Wells III would prefer it to be a spouse, and not someone you were just dating. Travis and I hadn't been dating when we started working here, so we had never had each other to lean on, not that we ever would have.

Because that would require trust, and that's not something I had with him.

Honestly, the only person I had truly ever felt I could trust while dating was my freshman year of college boyfriend. Or at least I thought I could trust him at the time. And then he had run away, pissed off when I'd beat him in classes and also hadn't wanted to deal with my health issues when I found out that the blood clots I was susceptible to were dangerous.

I was nervous about what that meant for this pregnancy, but the state of denial that I needed to hold on to so I could get through this work lunch and subsequent meetings meant that I wasn't going to focus on it. Or focus on the fact that more testing may be done, and I was going to have to be careful.

We made our way to the restaurant across the street, and Nathan's wife and her assistant were already there. Her assistant was a tall man with wire glasses and a soft smile.

"It's nice to meet you," Nathan's wife said as she introduced herself. "I'm Kelly. This is Jeremiah."

Jeremiah nodded at me and went back to his phone.

"Jeremiah is always working on a thousand things at once, even though I told him he's supposed to take his lunch off. One day I will take that phone and throw it."

"And you will get lost without your calendar."

She rolled her eyes before leaning forward to kiss her husband on the cheek.

"So, is this where we talk about girl power and we try to take over the world?" Kelly asked, and Nathan just sighed.

"I'd rather just take over the world. You know I love your girl power, but I don't think I'm allowed to be part of that club."

For some reason, I was completely relaxed. Even though there was a part of me freaking out, the dynamics between them felt right.

"Anyway, I wasn't sure what you wanted to drink or anything, so I ordered waters, and they should be here soon to get our actual lunch order. I know you guys have meetings to go to. And I have one with a friend of yours."

I perked up. "Oh?"

"I own a small business with a friend of mine, and I'm going to be working with Paisley Cassidy Renee. They do great PR, and their little matchmaking company on the side makes me happy. Seriously such a great company."

"You don't need matchmaking," Nathan grumbled as he looked over the menu. I just smiled.

"Paisley is the best. My best friend actually works for her too."

"Devney Cassidy? I always wondered if they were sisters."

I shook my head. "No, but it's a long story."

And not my story to tell. The fact that Paisley was the ex-wife of Devney's husband's twin, and Paisley was the ex-sister-in-law of my future baby's father, was not something I really wanted to contemplate. The tangled webs already woven were ridiculous, and I had a feeling they weren't even done.

"Oh, well it's not my business. I'm just glad that she's going to be working with us."

I smiled. "The company does fantastic work. I'd say they're the best, but I'd like to think *we're* the best."

Nathan grinned. "And we'll be even better with you as junior partner. So let's formulate some plans around how exactly to make that happen."

I put my hands on my lap, letting out a slow breath.

"That would be quick though. Right?"

"Yes and no, Addison," Nathan said after a moment. "I was a little older than you when I was promoted."

"You say that as if you're ancient," Kelly said fondly, and I smiled, though it felt slightly brittle.

"I want this job. This promotion. I know it's been whispered about for months, but I'm right for it."

"I know you are, that's why I'm backing you. But it's going to be a struggle. I have a feeling that Harrington is going to make his decision with or without the junior partners' say."

"That sounds reasonable," I said sarcastically.

"But we can persuade him, just like the others will try to. This upcoming event is going to be important."

"I know. I've been working on it for weeks."

It was a weekend retreat complete with meetings, presentations, and fancy dinners. There would also be hiking, and other "relaxing" events.

"I'll be going to that one," Kelly said as she met my gaze, and I could tell she wanted to say something else.

"What is it?"

"I am a woman in a high-powered position. And I married a man also in a high-powered position." She looked over at her husband and smiled. "And I know he works for an asshole who doesn't like women in the workforce."

"Kelly," Nathan warned, and I held up my hand to him.

"No, she's right. And I want to prove him wrong. I'm doing it just by being there and breathing."

Nathan sighed but nodded. "You're right. And it gets under his craw. Just like it does with Travis."

"However, the one thing you two have working for you is that you're both single. You don't have to compete with the whole family thing."

I frowned, not understanding.

Kelly continued. "If Travis shows up with a woman on his arms and a family on the way, he's going to get the job. Because Harrington-Wells III likes the idea of legacy. You showing up alone means that you're a strong woman, and you're putting your career first, however, you're also not the perfect legacy that Harrington wants."

I scowled, and nearly blurted out that I was all about legacy, considering what was currently happening inside my body, but I had barely come to terms with that, and didn't want to deal with anyone else's reaction yet.

"Kelly."

"I know, I know. And all of this is highly illegal and against the code of ethics, but we know how it runs. You know it, Addison."

"Are you telling me I'm supposed to just pull a fake fiancé out of the blue?"

Nathan cursed under his breath as Jeremiah snorted, still working on his phone, but Kelly gave me a serious look.

"I'm not saying make one up. I'm saying that this job will eat you alive if you don't have a support system."

"I do. I have my friends. You're working with them. I have a good family. And I'm damn good at my job."

"Good. Nathan has more balance at this position, so *when* you get this job, not if, know that balance is coming. So maybe figure out exactly what you want outside of that."

I wasn't sure what I was supposed to say to that. Did she want me to work hard and dominate, or get married and have the perfect practical life that Harrington-Wells wanted?

And how was I supposed to deal with all of this when I already knew my life was going to change—promotion or not.

Finally, the waiter came and took our order, then Nathan laid out our plans—for the retreat, what I needed to do with my current clients, and how I would make my way into this promotion. A promotion that would be good for everybody. For the company, for me, and whatever future plans I had.

By the time we made it back into the office, my mind was whirling, but I was still hyped up. This would be for the best. This would give me more time, more options, and I wouldn't have to work so many hours.

And then I could come to Luca with a perfectly formulated plan.

I could still hear the denial screaming in my head that I knew that this wasn't exactly perfect, but it was better than nothing.

It was more of a plan than I had that morning.

I made my way into the conference room for the next part of the project and nearly ran into Travis.

He looked good as always, his tailored suit cut to perfection. His shoulders were broad, his chest thick. He looked damn good in a suit, but he was like a snake in men's clothing, slithering and hissing when he didn't get his way.

"Oh, Addison, good to see you finally show up."

"I was at a work lunch, which I'm sure you know because you like putting tabs on me."

"No no, no need for that. My fiancée was just at lunch with her boss and told me you were there."

I froze, trying to understand exactly what he just said.

He couldn't be saying what I thought he had, right?

There was no way someone was stupid enough to want to marry Travis Armstrong. Then again, I dated him. The worst eight months of my life.

There was this ringing in my ears and my knees went weak, but it was fine.

Travis was getting married. Good for him. I wasn't jealous in the slightest.

But I couldn't help thinking about what Kelly had just said.

About the fact that Travis was going to look like the perfect family man on paper.

And I was the cold woman without a heart who had clawed her way to the top.

Neither of those were actually true, but the screaming in my head combined with whatever hormones that were now pumping through my body made me feel like I was a fucking idiot.

And I said the worst thing possible.

"I'm so happy for you. Congratulations."

"Dory will be at the retreat, and I'm really excited for her to really get to know the company and the family that we've made here. She's used to this type of thing though, since her father is Jackson Ford."

Bile rose in my throat, because Jackson Ford was a billionaire tycoon who made a shit-ton of money with our company.

Travis's fiancée was Dory Ford, the brilliant debutante who also made a name of her own, and somehow lowered herself to be with Travis Armstrong.

I knew it wasn't his dick, I remembered his dick. I bet it was that smarmy smile. Somehow that's what did it.

But I kept my smile on my face and hoped it wasn't too brittle.

"Oh, wow. Seriously, congratulations. I can't wait to meet her at the retreat."

"I'm sure."

And then it was as if someone had taken over my body, like I were a puppet on a string, and words were coming out of my mouth that I didn't approve, that I knew I needed to stop. But the words that I had jokingly said to Kelly poured out of me, and I made a fucking mistake.

"Seriously, I'm excited to meet her. And for you to meet Luca. My fiancé."

Travis blinked, then looked down at my bare fingers. I wasn't wearing a ring, because I had just made up a fiancé.

I'm such a damn idiot.

"Really? I didn't know the happy news."

"Congratulations."

I froze at Harrington-Wells III's voice behind me, and slowly turned, my palms going sweaty. If my morning sickness hit, I was going to throw up all over Travis.

But I plastered a smile on my face and looked at my boss.

"Oh, thank you."

"Look at that, our top two competitors for the promotion both getting engaged and bringing their future spouses to the retreat. As if this was kismet. I couldn't have written this script better myself. I cannot wait to meet both of your fiancés. I already know Dory's father, and he's such a great guy. I can't wait to get to know your fiancé too. Luca, is it?"

I nodded as Travis gloated about his fiancée.

He was probably really engaged to her. A real woman, with a real engagement, and a real engagement ring.

I was a liar. A big fat liar.

And now I needed to convince Luca to lie with me.

Oh yes. Because asking Luca to lie for me while we were still not talking about the very large baby-shaped elephant in the room was totally going to work out.

And as if on cue, nausea hit, but I ignored it.

Just long enough for me to break away and run to the bathroom and vomit up all of my mistakes and whatever I had eaten for lunch.

Luca was going to hate this.

I really needed to find a way to make him agree anyway.

I was screwed.

Chapter Five

Luca

"Thank you so much, Dr. Cassidy. I don't know what Rocco and I would've done without you." Mrs. Braverman reached out and gripped my hand. I smiled at her and the tiny teacup poodle in her arms. Rocco, adorable with his pristine haircut and wide eyes, lifted a single lip at me.

I smiled at the seven-year-old dog, knowing that if I blinked, the dog would try to rip my face off. Not because it was rabid or mean, but because it felt like it.

Rocco was a jerk, but he was cute. And Mrs.

Braverman kept the foul beast away from children and other small animals.

She did not keep Rocco away from large dogs who were just trying to protect their owner.

I loved the German shepherd out in the lobby, and Jones would soon be inside, shaking because he was afraid of needles, and I would take care of him too. But first, I needed to get Rocco out of the building so Jones was safe.

German shepherd, meet tiny teacup poodle from hell.

It was just my life.

"Now, let's get you out through the side door, so you can easily access your car."

"Oh, you're right. That would be smart. There are just such big dogs out there. And cats." She snarled the last word.

I made a non-committal noise, and we made our way out the side door. I had already handled the paperwork with her, as well as payment, so we didn't have to deal with any other animals.

I got Mrs. Braverman and Rocco safe inside her car, with Rocco giving me the evil eye over her shoulder the entire time. I was still behind a bit and had a full schedule. It didn't matter that I had gotten in early to get through paperwork and had worked through lunch—all I did these days was work.

"Dr. Cassidy? Jones is ready."

"Room four?" I asked. My tech smiled and pointed that way.

I walked to the door as she went off to do all of the things she did during the day to keep the place running. Colt and I needed to hire another admin, as well as take on another vet soon. We were both overrun and no matter what we did we could never catch up. We did have a friend we thought could handle working with us and, when he could, he covered for us so we could have this thing called time off. I hardly knew what that meant, however.

I was grateful for my team and for my partner. Colt was great at the business side of things, and made sure that we kept things running smoothly, but wasn't great at the whole people thing. Thankfully he was wonderful with animals, hence why he was here, but working with people? Let's just say I was glad for our vet techs.

And if I continued thinking about work, the fact that rent was due on the building soon, that we had countless insurance claims to work on, and we were overworked and overcapacity, I wouldn't worry about the fact that I was going to be a father.

I froze at the door, hand on the doorknob, and swallowed hard.

A father.

That didn't even seem real.

I never thought I would be.

Not after losing Ashleigh. Ashleigh and I had been together all through high school and into college. We had been engaged to be engaged for most of the time we were together. Promise rings and all. It wasn't until her sophomore year in college that we even slept together, something that my brothers teased me about.

It wasn't that I hadn't wanted to sleep with Ashleigh, it was that she wanted to wait until we were married. So we waited. And waited.

And I had gotten very good about masturbating—it was the only thing that kept me going.

The thought of being with anyone else when I was with Ashleigh never even crossed my mind. She was my everything. Of course, I finished college far too young and had been in vet school for four years right after. So my timeline of events might've been different than most college boys.

And then Ashleigh died from a brain aneurysm only a few months later. We hadn't had the future we planned or thought we deserved. Instead, I lost the woman that I loved, the woman that I thought I would have forever with. We were going to get married, have children, and have the perfect life that we always craved.

We were going to be Portlanders, with our funky little house and overpriced property taxes. We were going to eat crunchy granola and have a Subaru—it was everything we ever wanted. We climbed mountains together, skied down Mount Hood, laughed and joked around. We had done the Oregon Coast drive countless times, always stopping off at Depoe Bay for the saltwater taffy. We loved Oregon and loved each other.

And then she died, and I was adrift.

I hadn't realized until much later that Ashleigh had been my anchor, because I hadn't had one myself.

When my parents divorced the second time, I realized that parents getting married, getting a divorce, then getting married again wasn't something that happened to everyone.

My parents loved and hated each other, and they decided to pull a parent trap. My dad took August, Heath, and I, and my mom took Greer.

We had lost out on years of being with our sister and getting to know her. And when we became adults, and we found a way to finally get out from underneath the shadow of our childhoods and how we were raised, it hadn't been in Portland. No, it had been in Denver.

I had lost my anchor, my future, and Portland wasn't good for me anymore. I had nothing left there. I moved with my brothers to be near our sister, and it was the best choice for us.

I had been friends with Colt since vet school, and since he had moved back to Denver to be with his family, we started up a practice together. He was six years older than me, and had a lot more life experience, but I didn't mind. He was the grumpy asshole who got things done, when I was the one who felt like I was just starting to live, or maybe floundering a bit.

It didn't seem real. None of it did.

It was just supposed to be one night, one amazing night, one night we weren't going to talk about.

And now here we were, with the complications and consequences of our own actions.

And we would deal.

"Dr. Cassidy?" My tech looked at me and I waved her off.

"Sorry. I'm going in. Knock knock," I said as I walked inside, and Jones and his owner smiled at me. Seeing a German shepherd smile with all those teeth made me happy.

"Oh, Dr. Cassidy. I'm so glad that you're here. Jones doesn't whine as often for you." She leaned forward and knocked on the desk next to her. "Knock on wood."

"I totally understand. Hello, Jones, how are we doing today?"

Jones tilted his head and gave me a quizzical look before letting out a soft bark. Not the deep guttural tone I knew he could do that could rattle windows. But just a little quick hello.

I smiled wide and went to do my examination.

After shots and going over diet and exercise, because Jones was getting older but was still very active, we were done and it was time for my next patient, a three-year-old cat named Cupcake, and I was pretty sure she was part devil.

I loved her with every ounce of my being.

She was rowdy, hissed at me if I looked at her wrong, and absolutely hated if I wasn't petting her while we talked.

Cupcake was a female orange cat, something incredibly rare, but so beautiful. She had that orange cat tenacity, with the I-don't-give-a-fuck attitude that made me love cats.

It was hard for me to have pets at my house since I was never home, but I always had space for whoever needed to be there.

Right now my house was empty, because every foster I'd had found a new home and a loving family that could be there for them.

The senior animal that I'd been taking care of when I found out about the pregnancy was now with his new loving family, and I was making a family of my own.

I held back a groan at that, wondering when the hell that would actually start to feel real.

Addison was pregnant. Actually pregnant.

What the hell was I supposed to do?

How were we going to handle this?

We hadn't even handled the fact that we slept together. No matter what, I knew we were going to remain friends, because that was the only option. But how much did she want me to be involved? I knew I wanted to be. Full stop. No matter what happened, I was going to be a father and I was going to be in that kid's life. But I also wanted to be in Addison's life without making things complicated. What would happen when she started dating other people? Oh my God. She was going to date other people and that person was going to be this kid's father even though I was still around.

Thankfully I was in my office while having this slight meltdown and let out a long sigh.

"Stop spiraling, Luca," I told myself, and went to my coffeemaker, grateful that I had splurged on a mini espresso machine.

It was the best thing in my life. It was the only thing that kept me sane.

"Luca?"

I whirled and sloshed hot coffee on my hand.

"Fuck," I spat, and went to clean up the mess I just made, ignoring the burn on my hand.

"Oh my God, Luca, I'm so sorry."

Addison closed the door behind her, looking frazzled as hell.

She was a little pale, with that grayish hue that she had since we had found out it was morning sickness. She wore linen pants and a silk top that went together into this professional sexy businesswoman vibe. Not that I would say that out loud because we were friends and I wasn't allowed to tell her that she was hot.

I'd mentioned it before, but now it would be weird...right?

This is why sleeping with your friends was a bad idea. It left all these questions and no answers, and apparently left a baby in the middle of it.

An actual fucking baby.

I set down the coffee mug and wiped my hands on my pants.

"Did you just wipe your burned hands on your pants that I know has dog slobber on them?"

I shrugged. "Maybe? Are you okay? I have a ginger ale in the fridge if you want some."

She smiled, and when it reached her eyes I relaxed marginally. She was absolutely gorgeous when she smiled and meant it. Again, that was something I wasn't sure I was allowed to say anymore.

"That sounds wonderful. But we need to talk."

I raised a brow as I reached down into my mini fridge to hand her a ginger ale. "The last time we talked, you said that you were dealing with a thousand things at work and going to see your doctor and that I shouldn't go with you to this first one." Something that bothered me but I knew it was because she needed to put the truth of this in her hands until reality settled in. And truthfully, reality didn't seem real at all. "Is everything okay? Is the baby okay?"

She put her hand on her stomach, then looked around the office, as if afraid someone was listening in.

"The staff can't hear you through the door. Unless you scream. Please don't scream."

She shook her head, then took a sip of her ginger ale and huffed out a breath.

"The baby's fine, I guess? It doesn't seem real yet."

"Sit down," I said, gesturing to the small couch in the corner.

"I'm pregnant, not feeble."

My stomach twisted at that. "I still can't believe that we actually say those words out loud."

"I don't know if there's a *we* about it. *I'm* pregnant."

"We're going to say we for now because I did help get us into the situation."

"*We* did," she corrected, and we laughed at the ridiculousness of this conversation.

"So, funny thing."

I sat on the rickety table in front of her and was grateful when it didn't collapse beneath my weight.

"What exactly is so funny about what's going on?"

"Well, I may have made things worse."

I frowned. "Did you tell my brothers and now they're going to come and kill me? Because I figured I would be the one to do that and then you would have to bury the body and it would be a whole thing."

She grinned and reached out and patted my knee.

I adjusted myself, grateful that she had looked away because apparently just a touch on my knee could get me hard.

I really needed to stop thinking about her like this, because it was Addison.

My Addison.

Damn it. It was really hard to think when I knew what she tasted like.

"I didn't do that, but we're going to have to tell them

eventually. First though, I need you to bear with me when you realize that I fucked up royally."

"What did you do?" I asked cautiously.

"You know how I work with Travis and he's an asshole?"

I scowled. "I know about your ex."

She cringed. "Well, we're both going up for the same promotion."

"Damn, the promotion for junior partner? You've been working for that since you started. That's fucking amazing."

"I know, right? And if I get it, *when* I get it, it'll open up my schedule, so maybe this whole baby thing won't be totally insane." She held up a hand. "We will get to the absurdity of that in a moment, but first, my fuck up."

"Okay," I said cautiously.

We both worked far too many hours at our jobs. We had to come up with a plan, and actually talk about it, eventually. Damn it.

"So, the problem is that my boss, the guy who's going to decide this, is very set in his ways about what the perfect partner looks like."

"So, he's a misogynistic prick?"

"Yes, but that's not it. Well not all of it. Travis is engaged."

I frowned. "And that makes you sad? You're not still hung up on him, are you?"

She waved that off. "Not in the slightest. I wish him well. Or I wish him out of my life. I don't care, she can have him. It's more the fact that because Travis will now be a family man, he has one up on me, according to the boss. So I did a thing, a really bad thing."

I had an awful idea about where she was going with this, but I couldn't say anything. I needed the train wreck to come to me.

"They don't know about the baby," she added, and I didn't feel relieved about that like I think she thought I would.

"Okay," I said, drawing out the word.

"But I did say that I was engaged. To you. And that you're going to come with me to the work trip that I have in two days. You know, the one that's going to make or break my career? The one where I totally said I was getting married and I actually said your name and now you're going to have to come with me."

I blinked at her, marveling at the absurdity of this. Because of course she would. Why wouldn't we make this farce of our relationship even worse?

"Did you really just make up a fiancé for your job?"

She stood up and began to pace. I moved back to

give her space. I didn't say anything because I wasn't firing on all cylinders right then.

"Of course I did. Because it's so absurd and ridiculous. But I really need this job. I love this job. And this promotion's going to do amazing things."

"And what about the baby?"

"I don't know about the baby. I don't know how it's all going to work. All I know is that if I get this promotion, it'll mean things will be easier. I can make my own schedule, I can work from home, I can have the chance to come to the realization that I'm going to be a mom and you're going to be a dad and we're going to have to talk about that. And we will. But first, I actually have to get the promotion."

"And you need me to be your fake fiancé for that to happen."

"Yes. I know it's last minute, but will you marry me? At least for pretend. At least for the weekend."

I heard the words, and yet they didn't seem real, because this had to be a dream, not quite a nightmare, but one of those anxiety dreams when you were stuck at school and you didn't realize that you were enrolled in so many classes. I still had those to this day.

"That's not exactly the proposal I was dreaming about."

When she went pale, I cursed under my breath.

"Okay, okay, so we don't joke about the realities of our relationship, just the fake part. Got it. Do you need me? For real?"

"I really do. This will help. I promise. It'll make things easier once we actually deal with the reality that we're having a baby. Because if I don't get this promotion, I don't know what I'm going to do. And I just lied to my boss and everyone there. And now I can't back out."

I cursed under my breath again and did the math on how I could make this happen. I could, because I had a good team. And I would, because Addison was my best friend.

And she needed me.

And I was a sucker.

"Hell. Okay. What do you need me to do?"

She broke down in tears and threw herself in my arms. I just held her close and hoped we weren't making yet another mistake.

Knowing we probably were.

Chapter Six

Addison

"So, how are we going to do this?"

I looked over at Luca, who had driven us here, and sighed. We sat in his car in the driveway, the engine off, both of us having taken off our seat belts but not making another move to get out. There was an almost silence in the car, when the engine cut off but you could still almost hear the vibrations in your inner ear canal. It didn't make much sense, but the silence felt deafening.

"I feel like we keep asking ourselves that question."

We hadn't found any answers. We were going one

step at a time and ignoring the largest step, the one we should have considered first.

But I didn't want to trap him in this. I didn't want to force the conversation and force his decision.

I would rather be a single mom who had to figure out her life, where work didn't make sense and the emotions rammed at you from all sides, than force Luca to be by my side.

And I wasn't quite sure that I was ready to look into the details or complications of that yet.

There was seriously something wrong with me, but it wasn't time.

We had another obstacle to deal with first.

"I got the time off from work, thanks to my staff being amazing, and so we're on this trip. And they're going to want to know why. And by *they*, I mean my staff *and* my brothers and sister."

I turned to Luca and nodded. "So, we'll tell them I needed a fake partner."

"Fake fiancé," he said dryly, and I winced.

"It's ridiculous. I shouldn't have to fake a relationship in order to get a promotion. Who does that?"

"Patriarchal societies that we can't escape. However, we'll get through this part, and then we'll get through the things that matter."

His voice was raised at the end, and I nodded.

"Okay. That is what we will do. We will tell them about the ridiculous situation we're in with my work, but nothing else."

He raised a brow. "At some point they're going to notice when you start showing. But of course, we will probably have answers before that happens."

I opened my mouth to say something, and then nearly jumped out of my skin when someone rapped their knuckles against the window.

I turned to see August standing there, a frown on his face and a grocery bag in his hand.

"You two just going to sit there all night? Everything okay?"

His words were slightly muffled through the glass, but I could hear him just fine.

I waved him off and he took a step back.

"We'll talk soon," I said quietly to Luca, who shook his head because he didn't believe me.

I didn't believe myself either.

But if we talked, then everything was real. And nothing felt real at this moment.

So we would, eventually. Once we had more answers. And once I was done allowing myself to be afraid that he would leave.

Because he said he would be there, but what did "there" mean?

Luca again shook his head as I opened the door to get out.

"Everything okay?" August asked again, frowning as he looked at me, then over at Luca as he walked up.

"Everything's fine. Just a long day at work." I winced. "But you understand that, you have to deal with students."

"I don't know, I'd rather deal with high school students dealing with hormones and rage versus finance bros."

"Okay, you've got me there," I said with a hollow laugh.

August looked between Luca and I, brows furrowing, before he shook his head. "You know what, I don't want to know. Just, whatever it is, know that we're here."

"We're fine," Luca growled before he held out his hand. "Come on. Let's go inside. It's going to rain soon."

I looked up at the gray clouds, the dreariness settling in to match our moods, and nodded.

"You're right. Let's go."

Without thinking I put my hand in his and he pulled me towards the front door. I didn't miss August's curious look, though I ignored it. There wasn't time for that. There wasn't time for anything at this point.

Everything was about to change, monumentally. Or

perhaps it already had changed and I was just trying to catch up.

"You're here!" Devney said as she threw her hands up. She wrapped her arms around me and hugged me tightly.

"I'm so glad that you're here. Come on inside. It's just the six of us tonight. I hope that's okay. Greer and her men are off on a trip."

I still held Luca's hand, and I hadn't even realized I was, but as Luca and I were always close like this nobody really noticed, other than August. Probably because I was acting weird, not August. After all, Luca and I were constantly touching each other, near each other. Though we were just friends. We didn't even have benefits except for that one night, and now we had a very huge result from that benefit. Not that I was going to dwell on that tonight because we had other things to talk about first.

I suppose fake marriages came before real babies, although I didn't really want that bumper sticker on my SUV.

My SUV that would soon need a car seat and a baby carrier and I would need a bag to hold all the baby things. How would I make my office into a nursery, or should I move? Or would Luca want us to move in with him, or maybe just the baby with him and he would want full custody? No, that wasn't Luca. And he was also not the kind of guy to just run away.

We would be forever bound, and not just from our friendship.

Everything was changing and I couldn't keep up.

"Addison?" Devney asked, worry in her tone.

I quickly pushed thoughts of my own impending reality away and smiled at Devney. "Sorry. Long day."

"At work," August said, disbelief obvious in his tone.

Well, I didn't believe myself either, but I didn't need him to press so hard. Mostly because I had no idea what I was supposed to be doing in this moment.

Devney frowned between the three of us before gesturing towards the dining room.

"Come on, I'll pour you a glass of wine."

I bit my lip, because I wasn't ready to talk about the baby. I couldn't even talk about it with myself, let alone anyone else. But it was Luca who took care of it.

"She's driving me home tonight because she lost the coin toss, so I get the wine."

He smiled then, and Devney rolled her eyes.

"You know, that is probably a good thing. Don't you have an early day at the job tomorrow?"

I nearly tripped over my feet and frowned. "What?"

"Unless you have a set day off the next day where you

can recover from a single glass of wine, let alone how much you had at my birthday, you don't usually drink much at these things anyway. Because you're always working. I mean, I love that you're so great at your job, but you work more hours than any of us do, and that's saying something."

"Considering that many of us own our own businesses, pretty much," Heath said as he came forward, two glasses in his hands. He handed Luca a glass of red wine, and me a sparkling water.

"If you want something else just let me know. But I know you like this stuff."

I smiled, actually grateful for the bubbles to settle my stomach. And it wasn't just nerves this time. "Thank you," I said before I took a deep sip, letting the bubbles settle me.

Luca met my gaze as he sipped his wine, and I ignored the way his throat worked.

Why was I noticing Luca Cassidy and the way his throat worked as he swallowed?

Yes I had always found him attractive. He had always done something to me, but he had been my friend first. And I hadn't wanted to complicate that or ruin that friendship. It didn't help that our lives were so complicated and connected that even a couple who were formerly married were now forced to sit in the same room together and we all had to pretend we didn't know they were most likely fighting.

Because we were all friends and Paisley and August were doing their best to be adults about it, but it was still something we didn't talk about.

And it seemed that Luca and I were going down a similar path. Not precisely the exact same one, but close enough.

And speaking of Paisley, the other woman walked slowly into the dining room, her red hair pulled back into a chignon at the base of her skull. She had on a killer green dress with tall heels and looked fucking amazing. She also had her eyes on her phone, frowning as she typed what appeared to be a million words a second.

We all stopped to stare at her, because honestly, how could you not stare at Paisley? She finally looked up and blushed when she noticed all of us staring.

Paisley was always so sure of herself, so strong and confident, except when it came to a few things.

Like the man standing on the other side of me, and the fact that she was terrible at dating.

"Oh. Sorry. Work." The phone buzzed again and she looked at it, though her shoulders softened a bit and a smile played on her face.

"Not work," August grumbled under his breath, and

Paisley just shrugged before setting the phone down on the table.

"Yes it was work the first time, but no that was Jacob."

I raised a brow inquisitively. "And?"

"And we were setting up our next date. Look at that, a fifth date." She held out both hands and shrugged. "I can't stay for long, not because of my personal life, but because I have a meeting and a cocktail dinner to go to." She rolled her eyes. "I so love when clients add last-minute events. But it's okay. Hence the dress. I didn't dress like this for a casual dinner."

She walked over and hugged me tightly, and I hugged her right back.

"It's good to see you. And that dress is killer."

"I feel a little self-conscious in it, because I usually wear black, but the green works?"

"Green on a red head is sort of the whole point," Luca said, and there wasn't any awkwardness with them. I knew there was a little bit with Heath and Paisley, but considering that she used to be married to his twin, that made sense. August, however, wasn't saying anything. He just stood in the corner sipping his beer.

They were always cordial with each other. But I knew there was something there. I didn't know what that something was, either hatred or animosity, or something more.

But just as I wasn't going to think about Luca or talk about what truly needed to be talked about, I wasn't going to force the situation with them. After all, that would just make me a bigger hypocrite than I already was.

"Anyway, how are you guys?" Devney said. "We have appetizers out, and dinner will be served soon. Come on, let's talk about our weeks."

I looked over at Luca, who shook his head slightly. I saw Heath notice the movement, but I didn't say anything, and neither did he. Instead, we all went to the dining room and took our seats, our conversation moving from the bar Heath worked at and owned and operated, to a new upcoming project that Devney and Paisley were working on together.

"I'm so excited to work with these clients." Devney beamed. "Seriously, they're so great."

"I think so too. Although I am kind of annoyed that you're not coming with me to this event tonight with these other clients."

"Because I don't have to deal with them. That's all you. After all, you're the boss."

Paisley rolled her eyes. "I hate being the boss sometimes."

"No you don't," Luca said with a laugh. "I mean, the paperwork sucks, but that's why we have business partners and helpers and staff that actually know what they're doing with that."

"Yes, Nathan's not great with people, but he is great with paperwork," I added.

"It's really why you need that odd couple situation, so your opposite is there to pick up the pieces, and vice versa." He shrugged as he took a bite of the antipasto.

"I'm just glad that I don't have to make all the big decisions," Devney put in.

"You're the boss of your department though, so there's that," Heath added. "Making all the decisions is complicated, but I do like the freedom that comes with something that you own."

"As I can't own a school, I don't mind being a high school science teacher." August shrugged. "But you entrepreneurs can do your own thing." He looked over at me. "When are you going to be the big boss?"

I stiffened before I looked over at Luca.

"After all, you kick ass. I assume you already did the corporate ladder taking over the world without having to do espionage or some shit like that."

We weren't going to get any other better segue into what we needed to talk about, but it wasn't going to be easy. My stomach rolled, and I didn't know if it had to do with nervousness or being pregnant.

And I really need to stop thinking the P word because that was going to stress me the fuck out again.

"What is it?" Devney asked, frowning between us.

"Um. Well."

"I'm going on Addison's work trip in a day or so. Should be fun. You know all those finance bros that we just can't get enough of." He sipped more of his wine while everybody frowned at us.

"Why on earth are you going on that trip? I was pretty sure that Addison didn't even want to go on that trip," Heath asked.

I looked at Luca, who I realized wasn't going to help me here. He was already helping me enough. Great.

"I'm up for a big promotion, but in order to get that promotion, I need a husband."

Everybody stared at me. Paisley blinked a few times and then leaned back in her chair, shaking her head at me. "Harrington-Wells III strikes again?" she asked, her voice dry.

Everybody frowned, and I had forgotten that Paisley was working with Nathan's wife, and also worked in a similar sector. Plus, Harrington and Paisley were on the same level of entrepreneurship. I was pretty sure Paisley was doing even better than Harrington, not that I would tell my boss that, ever. I was already lying to keep my job, I didn't need to add harsh truths to it.

"What's going on?" August asked, leaning forward.

"I'm up for a promotion, but so is Travis."

"Asshole," Devney growled. "I mean Travis, not you. But both of you guys going up for the promotion? Is he going to try to cut your feet out from beneath you like always? He's always been conniving."

"He wasn't conniving the whole time we were dating, just at the end. Hence why he's not my boyfriend now. But yes, he's going to try. And because the junior partnership is something that brings in a new sense of responsibility, it also brings a different lifestyle." I shook my head. "I'm not saying this correctly."

"What she isn't telling you is the fact that Travis is engaged, and her boss really likes that Travis is now going to be part of a perfect family and is going to have the 2.5 kids with the happy adopted dog. So, what did you do about that, Addison?" Luca asked, raising a brow.

I knew he was trying to help, but none of this made sense or was making it easy.

"I told them that I was engaged, and I was going to bring my fiancé to the company work trip. Because that totally makes sense."

Everybody started talking at once, while Luca just sat back and stared at me.

"Are you kidding me? How's that legal?"

"Enforcing the legalities versus the perception are two different things," Paisley put in.

"It's fine, it's fine," I said, mostly to myself, though I was still trying to calm everyone down.

"It is fine," Luca said as he reached forward and gripped my hand.

Everyone stared at the gesture, and Luca sighed.

"We're just going to pretend we're engaged for the trip and then we'll figure out the next step. She needs this promotion, she deserves this promotion, and we're already best friends. What's a little fake engagement between friends?"

"I've seen that movie, it doesn't end well," Devney said flatly.

I grinned. "No, but the only other choice is to tell my boss that I lied because I was nervous and incompetent and going through too much. It's fine. I realize that there's not an easy way out of this, but we're going to stick with it for now. And we're going to kick the patriarchy and my boss in the balls, and then I'm going to get the promotion and everyone's going to forget the fact that I had a fiancé for one weekend."

Nobody looked as if they believed me, and frankly I didn't either.

There was really no easy way out of this, but I was

the one to put my foot in my mouth, and Luca was trying to save me.

So we would deal with this.

Even if nobody at this table believed me, even myself.

It didn't help that he was still holding my hand, and I didn't want him to let go.

The fake engagement thing was the easiest part. That was the part we could talk through.

The fact that I also wanted him?

That was the part I knew would twist everything.

But there was no going back now. And I was truly afraid there never had been.

Chapter Seven

Luca

The work retreat for Addison and her company wasn't during the best time for me. Thankfully, a friend of mine and Colt's had been able to step in and take care of the patients I had. But I didn't work seven days a week all the time, so I had actually been able to do this.

I would've done this for Addison even without the lie. Because she was my friend, and I hated her ex, and her boss, and her job. She needed me, so I would step up.

But the fact that we weren't actually talking about the elephant in the room was driving me crazy.

The event was at a huge lodge that catered to corporate execs and retreats for team building and bonding. I found it odd that they wanted families and spouses there, real and fake, but that was fine. If this is what Addison needed to get ahead, then I would help her.

But I knew she was using this idea of a promotion and beating her ex as a way to not think about what was actually going to happen.

"We're almost there," I said after a moment, and I realized the awkwardness in the car wasn't just on my end.

"You're right. And I've been so busy at work, and so have you, that we actually haven't made any ground rules."

I raised a brow even as I kept my attention on the road.

"What kind of ground rules are those, Addison?" I asked, trying to keep my tone calm.

She was pregnant. Having our child. And we weren't talking about it. If we didn't talk about it, I couldn't come to terms with it or make it feel real. Perhaps that was why we were doing this, but if this is what we needed to do for her fucking five-year plan, then we would.

I was not going to become my father or my mother. I would not be a deadbeat parent that left when things got complicated. I would be there. I just needed to figure out exactly what there meant.

"What's wrong?" I asked, looking at her briefly before tearing my gaze back to the road. "What do you think, Addison?"

"Stop saying my name like that. I know this is ridiculous. I know you put your life on hold for this weekend, and I'm so grateful. I owe you."

"You don't fucking owe me. We're best friends."

"Best friends are allowed to owe each other."

"Fine, then you owe me a conversation."

"I was trying to have one right now."

"How about a conversation about the fact that we're having a kid. An actual real-life baby. Not one that we can schedule at a time that is more convenient for us both."

"Luca..."

"What?"

"Let's figure out this whole retreat and the fact that we have to lie the whole time before we get to that part."

"And then we'll come up with something else to worry about, like the fact that what, Paisley and August are somehow not fighting? Or that something will happen with someone's job, or I'll get busy at work, or you'll get the promotion, and then there's a whole new set of issues. Life is always going to be in the way, but we created it. Actual life. Maybe we should talk about it."

"What do you want to talk about? We're having a baby. An actual baby. We're in the first trimester. I'm reading the books. Are you reading the books?"

My hands tightened on the steering wheel.

"I got the checklist of books we were supposed to read. And while I'm only a vet, I'm still a doctor. I know how pregnancy works."

"You're not an obstetrician, or a neonatal surgeon. You're not a fertility doctor. You help deliver puppies and kittens. Not babies."

"Fine, I get that. And I'm reading the books, Addison. But we're still not talking about it."

"I don't know what there is to talk about right now when we have to deal with this. This farce of a weekend." She put her hands over her face and let out a little growl. A damn sexy growl, but I didn't let myself focus on that.

"I'm keeping the baby."

"I know." My chest tightened because I was feeling that tiny spark of excitement. The need to know more about this baby.

Because this was real. Whatever happened this weekend, it might have some reality to it, but what was happening between us? That was real. Whatever that was.

Ever since that drunken night, I had wanted more. Fuck, I had wanted more before that night. But we had put ourselves in the boxes that said friends only, and I had accepted it. I lived with it because that made the most sense. It would screw up the dynamic of our friendship and our friend group otherwise.

But we were blowing that all out of proportion now, weren't we?

So, how did you tell your best friend and mother of your future child that you wanted to date her?

You didn't.

Hell, I was a complication here.

"So we read the books, we have this baby, and what?"

"And we raise this baby. I have more space than you, it just makes sense, right?"

"You're right. It does. And you're not doing this alone." I let out a breath as I took the exit off the highway. "We're going to talk about it more when we get back from this trip. I know that. But I want you to know that I'm here. I know that this part is real. And that we're going to have to tell our family and friends and then they're going to want answers we don't have."

"Then we'll ask the questions first. I'm just trying to

live in my bubble of insecurity and non-reality for a little while longer, okay?"

I snorted, shaking my head. "Well, panic with me, won't you?"

"Always. We're good at panicking together."

I sighed, then gestured towards the glove box. "Open it. I have a gift."

I was suddenly nervous, not knowing if this had been the right move or not. But if we were going to go along with the charade, we might as well lean into it.

She frowned at me before leaning forward and opening the glove box.

When she just sat there, not saying anything, I nearly pulled over.

"Addison?"

"There's a ring box in here."

"Yes. It's a ring. I figured it'd be a good idea to have one. Don't you?"

"You got me a ring."

Suddenly aware that I had probably stepped in it, I sucked in a breath.

"I'm not going to do this half-assed. We're going to get you that promotion so you have more time off and you get what you earned and deserve, and then we're going to celebrate. In order to do that though, I have to be the best fake fiancé ever. And that includes getting you a ring."

"Oh."

I scowled as I took another turn. "Open the damn box, Addison. It's not going to bite you. I'll bite you though if you don't. Just warning."

She blushed, and then I remembered our night together and how I did bite her.

Dammit. So not the time.

"Okay fine," she muttered, before reaching for the box. Suddenly nervous, I kept my attention on the directions and road rather than her.

When she didn't say anything, I cursed under my breath. Grateful for the stop sign, I turned and met her gaze, annoyed with myself for the whole damn situation. "What?"

"It's beautiful."

I was nervous again. This wasn't a real proposal, I knew that. But doing it in a car at a stop sign on her way to an event for her work when I hadn't even asked? This probably wasn't the best idea.

I quickly looked in the rearview mirror, and since I couldn't see any cars coming, I put the car in park.

"What are you doing?" she asked quickly and turned toward me as much as the seatbelt would allow.

"I wanted to get something that fit you. It's an

older ring, a little more unique setting, but that's a diamond with emeralds all around it. You look nice in emeralds."

She looked at me with wide eyes. "You got me a ring, Luca."

"You're my best friend, Addison. If I am going to be your fake fiancé, I'm going to do it right." I cleared my throat, then pulled the ring from the box since she hadn't. Feeling awkward as hell, I took her left hand and slid the ring on her finger. For some reason, that felt like an oath, a promise. Or perhaps it was just my dreams. After all, I hadn't let myself want her before.

"Addison Lily, will you fake marry me? Will you make me the happiest fake fiancé until the end of this farce where we can step into reality and realize that the real world is just as tough as this fake one? Will you make me a happy fake man?"

She blinked at me, her eyes going dark for a moment before she threw her head back and laughed.

"Fake man? Really?"

"I was leaning into it, and I went too far. So, what do you say?"

"The ring's on my finger, Luca. You're the one doing something real for me. But you did not have to spend that kind of money."

I shrugged. "I got it at a consignment shop. Like I'm

really going to go to a fancy jeweler and get you some nice shit. Sorry, I'm saving for a child."

We both froze as reality started to seep its way in.

"Oh dear God. There are child funds. There's child-care, and college funds, and prom and tuition and diapers. Oh my God, so many diapers."

"Okay, there's a car coming and we need to go, so push that off to the side. Remember, we're leaning into the fake."

"Sure. We can totally do this. Oh my God, breast-feeding. I'm going to need breast pumps."

My gaze went straight to her breasts, then back to her face.

"I can help with that."

I said it so serious that she blinked at me before she grinned and punched me in the shoulder.

"Asshole."

"I can also play with your asshole. You just tell me what you want."

She scrunched her nose and I laughed before I put the car in drive again and we made our way up the hill.

"This whole thing's ridiculous, you know," she said softly.

"I know. But don't worry. We can do this."

"You really got this at a consignment shop?" she

asked softly, and then I realized what she was asking. Why I might have that on hand.

I cursed as we made our way into the lodge, but I drove slowly so the valet wouldn't get to us right away.

"It's not... It's not hers." Hers as in Ashleigh's. Because we hadn't gotten that far. "It's also not a family heirloom."

Addison snorted. "I wonder how many wedding rings your mom has?"

"I don't ask those kinds of things," I said with a wince. "But don't worry, it's a real ring. For my real friend in this fake relationship. I wonder how many bingo slots we get for that."

"I don't even want to think about what the free space would be."

I laughed as we finally pulled into the valet.

Because this was it. The start of everything, and maybe the start of nothing.

I couldn't screw this up.

Because college tuition and daycare and car seats and diapers were on the way.

My breakfast that I had downed far too quickly earlier threatened to make an appearance.

I really didn't want this true reality.

Not yet. So I would lean into the dream and the acting. I had to.

By the time we were at the cocktail party that night, it felt as if I were doing a thousand things at once and yet running in place, much like the Scooby-Doo gang. Honestly I would much rather be hunting old creepy men in sheets pretending to be ghosts than dealing with this. Of course, I had plenty of the old creepy men at this event.

"Lily, come over here. Introduce us to your man."

I raised a brow at Addison because I had never once heard her called by her last name.

She smiled brightly and moved forward.

"Mr. Wells, this is Luca Cassidy."

Harrington-Wells III looked down pointedly at the ring on her finger and winked at me.

"Good job on the ring. I was a little worried that she was hiding you from us for so long for a reason. You're a vet?"

"Veterinarian," I said as I shook the man's strong hand.

"Ah, large animal or small?"

"Small animal, although I do have some experience with large animals because I did some work out in Portland on farms. But small animal here."

"Good to know. Had a cousin of the wife's that was a large animal vet. At least back in the day. Now he owns some property and uses it for dude ranching or something." The old man just rolled his eyes. "Not quite sure, but it works for him. So, Lily, when's the wedding?"

"Oh. Well."

I cleared my throat, wondering who this Addison was beside me, because this was not the woman that I knew.

"We're still waiting to plan, allowing for a bit longer of an engagement. You know, enjoying ourselves."

I put my arm around her and squeezed her hip. She looked up at me, and I tried to force her to understand that everything would be okay.

This had to work. It was the whole reason we were here.

When she smiled up at me and her shoulders relaxed, I saw a glimpse of the Addison that I knew.

"Yes, we're just enjoying the engagement for now. Plus, with the two new accounts, I'm focusing on that."

"Yes, yes. You've been doing good on that with Nathan."

"He's a great junior partner and I'm looking forward to working with him more in the future. With all of the partners."

"Ah yes. Oh good, there is Armstrong and his fiancée. I need to go meet that lovely woman again. Enjoy yourselves, the fun starts tomorrow." He winked as he said it, and I had a feeling that nothing about this would actually be fun.

She visibly relaxed when the man walked away, and I kept my arm around her, keeping her steady.

"So."

She shook her head, and then looked down at the sparkling water in her hand.

"I really wish this was booze right now."

I clinked my soda to hers and grinned. "I am in solidarity with you. Don't worry. I won't be a drunken mistake."

We looked at each other, and she blushed when I shook my head.

"It wasn't a mistake, Addison," I whispered, even though this was the worst time for that.

"Anyway, I'm really sorry about the bed situation."

I grinned at her. "They think we're engaged. Of course, there's only one bed in the room. It's a nice room though, a suite?"

She nodded. "There's a small couch, but I don't think it's even long enough for me."

"Addison, we're best friends and we've slept together. I think we'll be fine in one bed."

I winked as I said it, and she smiled before another group came over to talk to us. Finance bros and their wives that seemed bored as hell to be there.

There weren't many women that worked with Addison, and that bothered me. I was used to how Paisley worked, where it was a good mix of people. This seemed to be a little more old school, but now that the cobwebs had been shaken off, Addison was back to herself and kicking ass.

Of course, all I could think about was the fact that once we were done with this evening, we were going to be dealing with the fact that there really was only one bed. And I was going to be sleeping next to her.

Trying not to touch her like I was now.

This was already a fucking problem.

I didn't know what Harrington wanted, but if it meant that I needed to step up to the plate and be the best fiancé out there, I'd make it happen.

But I couldn't help but wonder exactly what this crew here would think once they found out that Addison was pregnant. Oh, there was nothing lawfully they could do, but there were always ways to make things difficult for her.

Would they really want a new female junior partner that was not only pregnant, but not even engaged? I didn't think so. I had a feeling that this was all going to be a problem for them, but Addison had always worked at the hardest colleges, on the most challenging degrees, and put herself up to be the best at the hardest parts of her job.

She was the best. I knew it deep down in my heart, even though it wasn't my career.

And as I watched her walk all over these finance bros without them even realizing it? I realized that she was a fucking star.

But these next months were going to change everything. And I didn't know how I was going to be able to protect her. I would do everything that I could, I would be there. But I was still just the best friend.

The best friend who'd put a ring on her finger, even if it was fake.

I couldn't help but think of Ashleigh in that moment, and I hated myself a little bit for it.

I had lost the one I loved before. Lost her to an aneurysm when neither one of us were prepared for that. But you never really could be prepared for something like that.

I couldn't help but think about the fact that Addison had medical issues of her own, and that was just one more reason I was keeping an eye on her. But I couldn't focus on that. I couldn't focus on the what-ifs. There were enough of them hitting me in the face as it was.

But every single little moment kept stacking against

us. Saying that this was going to be too much, and we weren't going to be able to find an easy way through this.

But what else was there? What were we supposed to do?

Addison Lily was fucking amazing. Stunning and powerful and brilliant.

I was going to do everything in my power to make sure she stayed that way.

Only I had a feeling that fate had already kicked us in the ass once, and it was going to do it again, and this was going to be a lot harder than I thought. Especially when her ex looked over at me and grinned, and I had a feeling that man was going to do everything he could to ruin this.

I kept my attention on Addison, and knew that we would kick that man's ass.

And hopefully get her this promotion.

Even though, no matter what, everything was going to change.

But we would do it. Side by side.

It wasn't like we had any other choice.

Chapter Eight

Addison

I had spoken to more of my coworkers in the past few hours than I had in the past few weeks. Usually, we stuck to our own departments, and while we did occasionally have meetings, both online and in person, it was usually small groupings. This was far different. I wasn't quite sure I liked it. But I knew that I was good at my job, and everyone here knew it.

We had done some team building exercises, including icebreakers, which made no sense to me considering all of us had known each other for so long that we shouldn't need to break any ice. However, whatever the boss wanted the boss got. I just needed to remind myself that this was for a good cause. For the next step in the plan.

So, why did it feel like nothing made sense?

Once dinner was finally over, we had our after-dinner cocktail, or at least everyone else was having a drink. That was when people got a little crazy, drank a little too much, and proceeded to have a little too much fun.

At least some people did.

I sipped my Virgin Cuba Libre, also known as a Coke, and smiled as my boss and my nemesis talked down to me. Of course, I snapped right back and stood up for myself. But it didn't always matter.

I had a sinking feeling that if I wasn't perfect, didn't do my job to the best of my abilities, I was going to lose out on this promotion. Because Harrington-Wells III loved Travis, and loved the connections he could make through Travis's fiancée Dory.

"Oh, Harrington, do you mind if I borrow Addison right quick?"

I looked over my shoulder as Kelly, Nathan's wife, walked up to us. "I have a business question for her, and I need that brain of hers."

"No problem, you can borrow Lily. We'll need her right back, though."

Kelly grinned and tugged me away.

"Is everything okay? Do you need me to call Paisley for something?"

Kelly shook her head as she waved at one of the wives who walked past.

"Oh no. But you looked two seconds away from strangling Travis, and murder's probably not going to get you the promotion."

I snorted and sipped more of my soda.

"Probably not, but I could try."

"You know you could. Now, I do actually have a question for you. How do you stand being called by your last name when you know he does it just to needle you?"

I shrugged, knowing that she was right.

"He does it to the guys too. So, it's not just me."

"He calls Nathan by his first name because he's junior partner. So I bet as soon as he starts calling you Addison, or Travis by his first name and not Armstrong, that's when you're going to know."

I cringed. "I figured that out and it sucks. It should be about what we bring to the company. What we can do for the team. And now it's all about politics."

"That's what most jobs are, even if they don't think it is. Now, speaking of office politics, who is that lovely young man you brought with you, because while that ring is gorgeous on your finger, it's so new you're still playing with it every time you get a chance."

I glared at her. "I don't know what you're talking about, Kelly."

"It's fine, you know. I know what it takes as a woman in a high-powered job. That's why Nathan and I don't work together. But we want to start a family, and doing that means we need to make sure we have the time and resources to do so."

Planning would've been nice, but as I gave her a brittle smile, I wondered how Nathan would handle that. Or would it be Kelly who put things aside in order for that phase?

Because for all this work towards a promotion, would it really help? Would I be able to find time to figure out exactly how to be a mom?

Would I be a good mom?

Bile filled my throat and I swallowed another sip of my soda, ignoring the fear that coated my tongue.

I didn't want to think about that. I couldn't.

"It's a new ring, but it's Luca. He's my best friend."

That wasn't lying to her, and I smiled, knowing it was true. Kelly grinned at me before reaching out to hug me tight.

"That makes me so happy to hear. You should marry your best friend. And he's a great guy. I mean, look at him. He's literally holding a kitten right now," she said dryly.

I turned quickly, nearly tilting off my heels as I saw Luca walk over, a tiny white kitten in his hands.

Every single wife and girlfriend and female in the vicinity came over to look at him and coo.

An odd bit of jealousy hit me, but that made no sense. This was Luca, women fawned on him all the time. I was usually his best wing man and would help him get the draw or push them away. Not that he ever actually went home with anyone. Which was weird, now that I really thought about it.

Or maybe he was still so hurt over his dead girlfriend that he was focused on that and not trying to go home with anyone else.

No, I was not going to let the inner voices scream at me tonight. I did not have time for a nervous breakdown.

Of course, all of that flew through the window when I looked at the man coming towards me with a smirk on his face and his hair falling over his eyes as he held a tiny kitten up to his chin and walked through the crowd of bystanders to stand right in front of me. I set my drink down, and looked up at him, my heart racing.

"Where did you get a kitten, Cassidy?" I asked teasingly.

He snuggled the kitten under his chin and shrugged.

"Found it underneath the deck over there. I only heard the one though, and I was going to go climb down to find more, but one of the staff members says that this is from the owner's daughter's litter. So we're going to go do a quick check and then make sure the kitten is reunited with its mother. They're weaned, but they're still pretty small."

He smiled and rubbed the kitten underneath the chin as it began to purr.

"Cute, right?"

"You're a menace." But I couldn't help it, so I reached out and let the kitten sniff my finger before it rubbed its tiny little nose against me. "Okay, this is so cute."

"Right? And I think that's the owner there, he looks a little harried."

I turned as an older man with a dark beard came forward, putting his hands in front of him, looking as if he were ready to pray.

"Thank you so much. This is Whiskers. He's the rambunctious kitten that got out of his enclosure." The man winced. "Not that we keep them locked up for long or anything, but it was bedtime, and it's not safe to have the cats run around when they're so small. Thank you so much for finding him. My daughter's distraught. We looked everywhere."

"He looks to be okay and healthy. Not dehydrated because he found that water bowl you have for I think strays?"

The owner nodded. "And any other animal that needs it. I'll make sure he's fed and everything. And I'll give him to our vet to check him out."

Luca held the kitten closer as it nudged his chin. "I'm a vet and don't mind doing another check over him, but he seems to be just fine. And I can point out the hole where the kitten got in, if that helps."

The man put his hands to his chest in gratitude as a little girl came running.

"Whiskers!"

The whole thing was like out of a storybook, and my heart began to race and my stomach tightened.

We could be having a daughter. Or a son. But a baby that wanted a little kitten to play with, who smiled just as bright as that little girl. When Luca handed over the kitten, I swore I heard women audibly sigh behind me.

I was right there with them.

There was nothing sexier than a grown bearded man holding a kitten as a little girl smiled up at him in thanks.

I was losing my mind.

And was very much attracted to my fake fiancé.

"I am going to go check on the kitten. Is that okay?" he asked, and I smiled.

"I'll come with you. The night's winding down."

"I'll say your goodbyes for you," Kelly said before nudging me gently, and I laughed, shaking my head.

"Thank you. It seems like the boss left anyway."

"Probably to find mistress number four," Kelly mumbled under her breath, and I rolled my eyes, knowing she was probably right.

Because for all the family values this man had, he was the worst kind of cad. The worst finance bro of them all.

I was a little bit better, but not by much. I didn't cad around like he did, I didn't lie and cheat, but I did kind of fly with the whole fake fiancé thing.

I wasn't going to let myself fall down that trap though.

I walked with the happy child and father at Luca's side as Luca answered 1,000 questions from the little girl. She wanted to know all about kittens and make sure that she was being a good kitten mom.

Luca was so patient, so kind. And when he went to go check on the mama cat and the other kittens, my heart raced.

There was seriously something wrong with me.

I had already slept with this man. I didn't need to

have all these feelings. That would just complicate an already very complicated situation, and we both knew that.

By the time we made it back to the room, I was tired and my feet ached.

"Get out of those heels, I'll go get us some water."

"You're too good for me. Seriously, I was just thinking about the throbbing in my arches right now."

"If you're good, I'll rub your feet."

I shuddered. "Not unless I'm just out of the shower. Feet freak me out."

He raised a brow at me and I rolled my eyes, sitting on the couch. I took my shoes off and let out a sigh of relief. I wiggled my toes as he handed me a glass of water.

"Really? So, you're not a foot fetish person. You do have pretty feet though. I bet I could take a photo or two of them and make some money. Maybe start a college fund."

I shuttered. "Oh gosh. No, I can't even think about that. And no, no foot fetish for me."

"Honestly same, though you do have pretty feet."

I looked down at my painted toes and shrugged. "For now. Who knows what they'll look like in the third trimester. I haven't gotten to that part of the book yet."

Lucas shook his head. "I don't know if that's in the book. I'm a little afraid to go to Google for images."

We looked at each other before bursting out laughing.

"You're right. That would probably be very bad."

"I'm glad I saved that kitten. It was a good distraction to an otherwise very odd evening."

"It was an odd evening. I hate these types of events."

"I'm just glad I don't have to do these myself. Although I'm sure there're veterinary conferences I can go to. I'll drag you along and you can be *my* fake fiancé."

"So you can get a fake promotion?" I teased, shaking my head.

"Maybe."

"Thank you, though. For tonight. For the whole weekend. I know it wasn't easy for you to juggle your schedule. And I know that this whole thing is annoying as hell. But I appreciate you."

Luca reached out and squeezed my hand. His eyes closed as he rested his head on the back of the couch. "Honestly, this is like a vacation from work. I love my job. Even when it finds me on trips like this. But it's nice not to have to be the boss all the time."

"But you're good at your job, you know. You made that little girl's day."

"They would've found the kitten eventually. But I'm glad I found Whiskers."

"I'm going to take a shower just to wash off the day. And then sleep?"

"Sounds good. I'll shower after you do. Then we have the lovely drive home in the morning."

It had been a long weekend. And while we had done well sleeping on opposite sides of the bed so far with a pillow fort between us, I knew we were being ridiculous. Because as soon as we left this moment, reality would set in and we would have to face facts.

Face planning.

I sighed.

"You did a good job this weekend."

"It doesn't feel like it. It feels like I'm losing."

I wasn't sure exactly what I meant because it could have been anything, but Luca took my hand to his lips and gave me a kiss. I swallowed, my mouth going suddenly dry, and I pulled my hand away, quickly standing and making my way to the bathroom without saying anything else. I pinned my hair on the top of my head before showering quickly. I didn't need to wash my hair, just wash the day off. I slid on my pajama bottoms and tank top, not the sexiest thing in the world, but I didn't need to be sexy. I just needed to be comfy.

Because hopefully our fake relationship would end

soon, and we would come to terms with just being friends again.

I gripped the edge of the sink. Yes, that would be good for everybody.

I brushed my teeth, then made my way into the bedroom. Luca was turning back the bedsheets when I entered and gave me an odd look before shaking his head. I didn't bother to ask what he was thinking, because I didn't want to know. And then he passed by me, his arm brushing mine and sending shivers down my spine. He shut the door behind him and then the shower went on, and I couldn't help but listen to the sound of water and imagine it sliding down his naked body. His hands over his skin as he lathered up the soap.

I licked my lips, then cursed myself before jumping into bed.

Well, if that was what he was thinking about when I was in the shower, no wonder he gave me that look.

And no wonder I was losing my mind.

I turned off the lamp on my side then lay on my back, blankets up to my chest, hands down on either side of me, willing myself to fall asleep before he got into bed.

I hadn't bothered with the pillow fort, but it would be fine. We were adults. We could do this.

The shower went off and I thought about how he

was naked in there, probably rubbing himself down with a towel, and it wasn't any of my business. He wasn't any of my business.

When he came out in his boxers and a T-shirt, I quickly closed my eyes and pretended I didn't see him. That I couldn't feel the heat of him as he slid into the sheets beside me.

When he shut off the lamp without another word, all I could hear were our breaths and, based on the rapid breathing, realized that neither one of us was calm.

Then his pinky touched mine and I shivered.

"Luca."

It was just a simple touch, a caress of pinky to pinky. And it was so much.

My clit pulsed, and I wanted to press my thighs together, to will myself not to come at just a simple touch.

This had been bubbling up for far too long. The need. The change.

But maybe I was just losing my mind.

Maybe it was the hormones. The lack of sleep. The stress. Maybe it was everything except what I was feeling.

"Addison," he whispered, and then his fingers were sliding up my arm, and I turned to him and opened my eyes.

"Luca."

"Let me kiss you."

We knew that this was a mistake and I didn't care. Because his hands were in my hair and his mouth was on mine.

He tasted of mint and smelled like the same soap I had all over my skin.

I wanted him. I needed him.

It started as just a simple touch, a caress, and then it was far too much.

His hands slid under my tank top, over my hips and my ribs, and I shivered when his thumb brushed the underside of my breast. I licked at his tongue and bit down gently on his lip as he slid his thumb over my nipple.

"You feel so fucking good."

"I was going to say the same about you," I whispered against his lips as I moved my hands up and down his body, and then under his shirt. His skin was so hot, still damp from the shower.

And I wanted to lick every inch of him.

We kept exploring each other, kissing, touching, and when he cupped my breasts under my shirt, I groaned, arching into him.

"Your nipples are so sensitive."

"More so than before," I whispered.

He kissed me again and we didn't talk about anything important or why I was so sensitive. I was on my back and he was tugging off my shirt. I did the same to him, and I was grateful for the moonlight sliding through the blinds, because I could just see the light on his skin, barely glowing, and he was so beautiful.

He kept kissing me, before he lowered his body down further, kissing along my jaw and in between my breasts. He suckled one nipple, then the other, pressing them together as he continued to kiss and touch. I just let my hands fall over him, needing to touch him, needing to tug on his hair. He kept exploring. And when he kissed his way down my stomach and began to pull off my pants, I let him.

I hadn't bothered with underwear and he groaned, tossing the pants over his shoulder, before he was cradled between my thighs, gently leaving small kisses on the inner silk of my skin.

"Luca."

"Let me taste you. Let me take care of you."

"Just please put your head between my legs right now. It is the sexiest damn thing."

He chuckled roughly against me, and I could feel the hot air of his breath against my pussy.

"I'm going to taste this cunt of yours, and I'm going to lick and I'm going to suck. And then you're going to come on my face and you're going to scream my name. And then I'm going to do it again and again until you're shaking and all you want is my cock."

He looked up at me and I swallowed hard, my pussy clenching just at his words.

"Do you want that, Addison? Do you want my cock? Are you greedy for it?"

I was already so wet, and I knew he could see, could practically taste.

"I want you."

"Say the words. Say you want my cock, Addison."

I bit my lip, slightly embarrassed, but I didn't care. Because Luca Cassidy was between my legs and I wanted to come so badly.

"I want your cock. Please."

"But first, you get my mouth."

And then he lowered his head and began to suck and lick.

I shivered at the exploration, at the way he spread my lips and began to breathe softly along my clit. I shivered, my toes curling, and then he was sucking and eating. His tongue was a masterpiece and knew exactly how to twist and turn. And when he slid one finger deep inside me, finding that bundle of nerves, I shot nearly off the bed. He pressed his free hand on my lower stomach, pinning me down as he continued to suck, to eat. I knew I was wet and I was hot and I was so close to coming.

Then he twisted his finger again and I was coming, shouting his name as my toes curled, and I nearly rocked off the bed again.

But he didn't stop there. He continued to suck, continued to lick, and somehow I was coming again, and it didn't make any sense. I was not the kind of woman to have multiple orgasms, but here I was, coming on Luca's face for a second time, and I didn't fucking care.

When he crawled up my body and crushed his mouth to mine, I could taste myself on his lips, and it was the most erotic sensation of my life. I was moaning words that I couldn't even understand as he was tugging off his pants.

His cock was thick and hard and there was already pre-come at the edge.

He met my gaze, and I realized there was no need for condoms, because we were both clean, we had made sure of it, and I couldn't get pregnant again.

But I quickly pushed those thoughts out of my mind because I didn't want reality. I wanted Luca right now.

Before I could do anything, he sat back and lifted me up with just his arms and core strength.

My eyes widened, and then he was sitting and I was straddling him, his cock pressed against my pussy.

He groaned before he gripped both sides of my face and kissed me.

"I'm going to lift you on my cock and then you're going to ride me. I want you deep and hard. Can you do that? Do you want me to fuck you?"

I nodded.

"I want the words. I need the fucking words, Addison."

"Fuck me, Luca. Please."

"As you wish."

And then he lifted me up by spreading my ass cheeks and slammed me down on his cock.

I shouted his name, my whole body shaking at the near orgasm. I was already so tight from my own orgasms that it was almost painful. He stretched me to the brink, but it was so damn good that I had to curl my toes just to not come again.

He lifted me up and down on his cock. I leaned back and put my hands on the bed to steady myself. And then I was moving with him, both of us fucking each other at an angle that meant he could use his thumb on my clit, nearly sending me over the edge again.

When sweat began to slide down my body, he gritted his teeth and pulled out of me, and then I was on my hands and knees and he was pounding into me from behind.

I gripped the bedsheets, pulling them off the mattress, and his hands were on my breasts, then on my hips. And when he slid his middle finger over my clit again, I came, clamping around his dick.

He pounded into me over and over again, the speed increasing until he was finally coming, roaring my name as he hovered over me, both of us shaking.

He kissed the back of my neck and then my shoulder, and then we laid there, my back to his front, his cock still buried balls deep within me.

And I looked at the mess we had made of the bed and laughed.

This was so ridiculous, and we both knew it.

He chuckled with me as he held me close, and I knew we'd talk in the morning.

We had run out of time not to.

But first, I was going to relish in this.

Because this had been the best sex I'd ever had.

And it was with my best friend.

I had no idea what I was going to do with that.

Chapter Nine

Luca

I liked Addison's house. It was homey, comfortable, and yet spacious enough there was never clutter. She had gone with earth tones to decorate, which was a change from what most of my friends had for their homes. She had done away with the token millennial gray on her walls, although my house was more of that color just because it was what had already been there when I moved in. But she had four screen walls in the living room because she had such large windows on the side that faced the mountains and it lit up the whole room. She had decorated the house with mustard yellow and royal blue accessories, and each room looked perfectly bohemian, with a touch of hipster, and a touch of princess as well.

It fit her, and I loved being here.

I loved the large kitchen, and had cooked there a few times for just the two of us, since we were friends.

I felt at home here, which was odd because Addison and I hadn't truly known each other too long. But as soon as we met we had clicked, and here we were. Things changing, irrevocably. Just like they always seemed to.

"I am all unpacked," Addison said as she entered the living room wearing linen pants, a crop top cotton tee with no bra, and I knew that because it was slightly chilly in here, and her hair loose and flowing to her shoulders. She had washed off her makeup while I made a quick dinner in her kitchen, using whatever she had on hand—a lemon sauce linguini with extra garlic. It wasn't enough protein for her, but we both loved pasta so it was going to have to be enough.

"Good. I am glad you got your shower in. I know getting sick on the side of the road wasn't your idea of fun."

She winced, shaking her head. "I'm sorry about that. Thank you for pulling over though."

I raised a brow then slid her plate across the kitchen

island. "I'm just glad that you didn't vomit on me. Though this probably isn't the best dinner conversation."

"Thank you for cooking. Seriously." She ducked her head, blushing. "You really are good at it."

I shrugged and took a bite. It needed a little more pepper, but I didn't feel like getting the pepper to add it.

We ate in silence. Neither one of us even bothering to sit. Morning sickness had been hard on her, and I was glad that she was able to eat. Maybe if I kept stuffing my mouth with food, then I wouldn't think about the fact that we needed to have a talk.

Because we shouldn't have done what we had the night before. Or maybe we should have.

We needed to actually talk about our feelings and figure out what the fuck we wanted.

But of course, that would mean I would actually have to know what that was, and that wasn't going to happen in her kitchen over linguini.

But I wanted to know.

I needed to know.

"We should talk."

I hadn't even realized I had said the words out loud until she looked up and swallowed hard, a little piece of cheese on her lip.

Being the idiot that I was, I leaned forward and

wiped her lip with my thumb.

"You had cheese."

"Oh. Right. Yes, we should talk. Here. I just thought we'd have a few more minutes. But then something else would come up and we'd put it off."

"We both know that's true. We're good at procrastinating."

She nodded, then looked off into the distance. "Thank you. For this weekend."

I raised a brow and she blushed. "Not for that. I mean, yes for that too. Because no matter what else happens, just know that you are amazing at that."

I nearly puffed out my chest. But I was better than that. Marginally.

"Addison."

"Thank you though. For real. For this whole weekend. For just being you. Because no matter what happens, no matter how many crazy moves we make or whatever slams into us from now on, I know that no matter what, I could only do this with you. You're Luca. You're steady and you're amazing and you're a rock. And I feel like a frantic mess who is trying to catch up, but you are so steady."

"You call me steady one more time, I'm going to throw you over my shoulder and show you exactly how unsteady I feel right now."

I hadn't meant to growl the words, and when her eyes widened I nearly cursed myself.

But I couldn't, not just then.

We needed to talk, we needed to get this out.

"We're going to have a baby. It's real, and somehow we're going to have to make this work. But no matter what, we have to make sure that we don't screw up who we are."

I had a feeling we had already done that, especially after last night, as there would be no coming back from that.

But maybe screwing up who we were didn't have to screw everything up completely.

Maybe we could change into what we needed to be.

Though I needed to figure out what that was.

"Okay. So we do this together. No matter what happens, I'll be there. Sonograms, doctor's appointments, helping you figure out what to wear for maternity clothes—all of it. I'm going to be there for first steps, first days of school. Everything."

Because no matter what happened, this was my best friend and we were bringing life into the world. This was it.

We were going to have a child. No amount of pretending that didn't exist was going to help.

And I would not abandon my child like my family

had abandoned us.

I knew Addison had grown up with a relatively normal set of parents. Parents who loved her and cared for her and didn't treat her like she was in their way. She had a solid base and had turned out to be a strong, confident, and terrifyingly amazing woman because of them.

My brothers and sister and I had come out who we were despite our parents.

But we were okay.

I knew that.

I just needed to prove it to myself sometimes.

"Of course, I know you're always going to be there. But..." She let out a breath. "We can never sleep together again."

My eyebrows rose and I shook my head.

"We can't really take back what happened last night, or the night that brought forth this lovely little complication."

Addison ran her hands through her hair, then started doing dishes. I grabbed a towel to start drying, both of us in sync as if we'd done this thousands of times. It was practically domestic.

But we had been friends first, and that was the hard part to remember.

"Sleeping together last night was a mistake."

I held back a flinch, but I knew she was right.

It made things far more complicated, far more twisty. We wouldn't be able to act rational like we both needed if we kept letting feelings and hormones get in the way.

"And I know that this is going to be hard, especially when our family and friends find out." She winced. "Oh my God, we're going to have to tell our family and friends."

I winced as she handed over a plate so I could dry it. "Yes. My brothers are going to kick my ass."

"Excuse me? I'm the woman who deflowered their baby brother."

I scowled. "I wasn't a virgin before we met, you know."

Clouds filled her eyes, and I could have cursed for that. Then again, she just used the word deflowered.

"I know. But you are still their baby brother. And I'm just the crazy best friend who slept with you."

"I'm pretty sure we slept with each other. More than once. Remember? I'm the one who told you to take my cock. And you're the one who greedily accepted."

"Luca Cassidy, don't say things like that. It's hard to think when you do."

"Well, we were thinking pretty well last night, weren't we?"

"That's why we can't do that again. It makes things

too complicated. We're already a tangled mess, and we can't be our rational selves and figure out what to do next with all of this if we are too busy worrying about sleeping together again. So we're not going to do that, ever."

I raised a brow. "So, we're going to raise this child as friends, with what, both of us having separate lives and dating other people and pretending that we're okay with that?"

I hadn't meant to say it like that, I didn't even know if us dating was the right move, but I didn't want to throw it away. To toss out just the idea of it because it was too hard.

"Luca, I just, I've never allowed myself to feel like that for you. I never wanted to lose your friendship."

"Don't put sex off the table. Because if we do that, it's going to make things worse. We're adults though. We can do this."

"Okay, but we're going to be friends first, no matter what. Because that is worth more than anything. Orgasms are great, but friendship is more. As is the fact that we're going to be raising a child and it's going to change everything. It's going to be so fucking ridiculous. I need to make sure that you are on board with this. That you are on board with midnight feedings and the fact that our lives are going to completely change."

"I'm there, Addison. I've been there."

"Okay. I know you're always there."

I wanted to curse at that, at the fact that it sounded as if it were my own epitaph, but I didn't. Instead, I just reached out and cupped her face.

"One step at a time. Telling our friends and family is a big step. And then doctor's visits, and work. But, Addison? I care about you."

There was something here, something I couldn't just ignore because it was difficult. I knew she wanted to, that she felt like she needed to ignore it. But fuck that. I wasn't going to let her walk away and put me in a box because she was scared.

Because I cared. I wanted to know her. I wanted more.

I just hoped that she didn't hate me in the end.

"Luca, I care about you too."

"Don't Luca me. We're going to tell the family, and then we're going to figure out when the next doctor's appointment is. I'm going to be there, no matter what. I'm not going to date anyone else. I'm not going to bring anyone else into this. It's just you and me, Addison. You're my best friend, that's just the way it's going to have to be."

I knew she was scared, but hell, so was I.

She had so much going on in her mind, so I had to be the one to step up first. To lay the groundwork.

I just hoped like hell I was doing the right thing. But when she didn't tell me no, when she didn't back away, I counted that as a win.

At least until the next step, which would probably ruin everything.

"So, when do we tell the family?"

"Soon. Though it's not going to be easy."

"I know."

"I'm not going away, Addison. So you're stuck with me."

I didn't add the word forever, though it felt to me as if it were screamed in the distance.

Because no matter what, we were connected forever.

In two trimesters, everything would change again.

I just needed to make sure she knew how much I cared.

That, hell, I wanted more.

Shit. I hadn't realized that until this moment.

That was something I was going to have to deal with.

All the while, seeing if the woman in my arms could maybe want me back.

That wasn't going to be difficult. Not at all.

Chapter Ten

Addison

Okay, dinner was set, the covered dish was ready to go. And I was ready for this.

I cringed at my internal pep talk, because it sounded as if I didn't even believe myself. And I probably didn't. Today was the day I was going to tell my friends I was pregnant. Because there would be no hiding it soon. My morning sickness that wasn't exactly morning but randomly inappropriate at times sickness was now abating slightly. But my pants were getting a little too tight, and I wasn't going to be able to hide the pregnancy for much longer. Not to mention I wanted to talk with my friends about it. I wanted them to know what was going on. Not that I knew exactly what was going on, but I wanted people other than Luca to talk about things with. I needed to talk to somebody rational. Because while Luca could be rational, he was also very much tied to his emotions.

I wanted someone to be able to tell me what to do or to explain that what I was doing was the right call. Which didn't make any sense, because I was usually great at making choices for myself.

I wanted to talk to my best friends. Because every time I talked to my other best friend, Luca and I added more complications and stress to our relationship. It made sense though. Because this wasn't just a one-off thing. We would be forever and irrevocably tied. And while at one point that wouldn't have bothered me because I would assume we would always be friends, as I would always be friends with his brother's wife, it didn't mean that I was ready for any of this. Everything had changed. And I needed to talk to my girls about it. I just wasn't quite sure how they would feel about this new turn of events. Because it would change everything. We wouldn't mean for it to, but it would alter the fabric of our group and our lives.

That wasn't overstating it at all. I wasn't overreacting. I was freaking the fuck out just like I should be.

I would get this over with, I would tell them, and they would either judge me harshly, freak out right alongside me, or something in between, but at least then they would know. It would be out in the open, then tomorrow I would tell my parents.

I just hoped they wouldn't be disappointed in me.

I shook my head and frowned. My parents had never been disappointed with me. Yes I had made mistakes in the past, because I was human, but they had always been there for me. They loved me.

And now I was going to make them grandparents.

I went lightheaded at that and had to lean on my kitchen island to remain steady.

My parents would be grandparents. What would they want to be called? Nana and Papa? Gigi and DeeDee? Grandpa and Grandma? Maybe a more formal Grandfather and Grandmother? I wasn't sure. We had never discussed it. Yes, we had always made references about future grandkids and me being a mom, but as I had never been in a serious relationship before this—not that I thought that this was a serious relationship—we had never seriously discussed any of it. It hadn't felt real. I didn't even know what they would want to be called. That seemed like something we should have talked about, but I wasn't even sure how they were going to react to knowing that their only daughter had gotten knocked up by a man during a drunken one-night stand. Although, could it really be called a one-night stand anymore when we'd had sex again?

I groaned, putting my head in my hands.

Oh, it had been so much more than a one-night stand. And we were both being very good about pretending that it couldn't be anything else, even though part of me could only think about that.

There was truly something wrong with me, and I didn't know how to fix it. I would blame it on the hormones, but I had been having this attraction to him long before that. Hence my problem with myself.

My parents were going to be grandparents. And so were Luca's.

I frowned in concern at that thought. Not for myself, but for Luca. I didn't know everything that occurred in his childhood, nor Greer's, but I knew enough. I knew that their family had been ripped from each other more than once, all because of the selfish wants of two people. Two people who hadn't cared about their own children, let alone anyone else other than themselves. And even then, I knew they didn't care about each other. They only cared for moments of time before they changed their mind. I didn't know how they could do that. And I vowed right then and there I wouldn't do that to Luca. Even if, no, even *when* we realized it would be better for us to only remain friends who raised a child together, we wouldn't pit ourselves against each other and put our child in the middle. No matter what, we would make sure that never happened. Because I trusted Luca with my life, and with my future. Maybe not my heart, but that was fine. I didn't need that. I just needed him to stay, and to not be broken in the process.

The doorbell rang, and I quickly pushed those thoughts out of my mind. I needed to tell my friends what was going on, probably with explicit detail about how it happened, because that's who we were, and I wasn't quite ready for that.

But there was no going back now.

I opened the door to see Paisley and Devney standing there, both smiling at me. Devney looked absolutely radiant. Of course, she usually did. That's what happened when you were in love and happy and things were working out for you. She deserved it. After all the tragedy of her life, and trying to figure out exactly who she was, she deserved to find that happiness. I loved that for her. And I loved how absolutely stunning happiness looked on her.

Paisley stood behind her, still smiling, still radiant, but not quite as happy. There was always something about Paisley that spoke of sadness, but I could never figure out why. I may have gotten to know Paisley well over the past year or so, but I didn't know all of her secrets. Like why she and August had divorced, or how she felt about the fact that she was forced to see her ex often, and in the face of Devney's husband—considering that the two were twins.

There was no hiding from your past when it literally stared you in the face.

"We're here. Sorry we're late."

I smiled as I shook my head.

"You're not late. I feel like I got ready early. I can't help it, that's just me."

Devney grinned. "True. But that's fine. That's why we love you."

I moved back and took the dish out of Devney's hand as Paisley came in holding a bag I assumed held dessert. We set everything out and found ourselves sitting around the kitchen island, talking about our days while I ignored the screaming inside my head.

Devney kept bouncing on her heels, looking anxious and excited all at once. I met Paisley's gaze, who shook her head. Apparently she didn't know what was going on either.

"I'm so glad we're doing this. I know it's not easy

getting time away from your computer and your files to do this with us, but I'm so grateful that you are."

I smiled again at Devney and tilted my head, studying her.

"Of course. Girls' night is the best thing that we do. I love spending time with you guys."

Would girls' night continue like this once the baby came? Would things happen the way it always had or would it all implode? We'd have to find a way to make it work. That was the whole point of this, but everything was going to change. I knew that, and they would know soon as well.

I just wasn't ready.

"So, what are we having for dinner?" Paisley asked, looking over my shoulder towards the kitchen. "Whatever it is smells good."

I had been in nesting mode, because I had been nervous and frantic.

Luca always made fun of me for that, because when I got nervous I began to cook, even though I wasn't really great at it. He was better, and we both knew it.

But there were a couple of things I could make really well.

"It's a spinach lasagna, which I know sounds disgusting, but there's so much cheese in it, five cheeses to be exact, that you can't even tell it's meatless."

"That sounds amazing."

"I also made garlic bread, and I have an Italian salad ready to go, and I have some appetizers."

"I brought those stuffed mushrooms that we plopped in the oven, they should be ready soon." Devney looked at her watch. "In fact, they should be ready now."

We went to pull them out, and the scent of yummy Italian food and mushrooms filled my nostrils.

"Okay I'm going to eat this entire tray of mushrooms," Paisley said with a laugh, and I waved her off.

"No, mine. All mine."

"Excuse me, the pregnant woman should be able to get to her food first."

I nearly opened my mouth to say of course that was why I was standing there, and then I realized exactly what Devney had said.

The pregnant woman.

But she didn't know it was me.

I turned to her, eyes wide as Paisley stood next to her, also staring at Devney, but Paisley's eyes were filling with tears, and the other woman put her hand over her chest, a smile playing across her face.

"Devney?" she asked, that smile growing.

I just stood there blinking, trying to come to terms with what had just happened.

Because there was no way Devney had just said she was pregnant, not today. Today was supposed to be the day I announced I was pregnant.

There was no way that Devney and I would be pregnant at the exact same time. Fate wouldn't be that ridiculous. Then again, maybe fate was exactly that ridiculous.

"You're pregnant?" I asked, my voice slow, unsure.

It wasn't as if I was upset. No, far from it. I just felt confused. And anxious, and happy. And sad. Everything all at once.

Because if Devney was pregnant, that meant our babies would be growing up together. They would be cousins, and they would be family.

And one of my best friends would be going through this pregnancy alongside me.

Even though she was married and happy and probably either planning or expecting something like this with her husband.

When I was the exact opposite.

I did all this thinking in the matter of milliseconds, when Devney put her hands in front of her, and squealed.

"I didn't know how to tell you, so I figured I'd do it with a joke. But yes I'm pregnant. And I want those mushrooms."

"Oh my God. You're pregnant? This is amazing. Congratulations to you and Heath." Paisley threw her arms around Devney and held her tight, while I stood there, a genuine smile on my face, but feeling two steps behind.

Because I wasn't sure what I was supposed to do now.

Of course, Paisley kept talking, giving me a moment to catch up with the rest of reality.

"Okay. When is the due date? How far along are you? And yes I realize that they're similar questions, but I literally cannot do baby math. So tell me everything. Oh, I know we had been talking about expanding the daycare center within the company, but we're going to have to do it now. There's three of you that are pregnant, and Sam's wife is also pregnant. And while his wife is going to be staying at home for a little while, eventually he'll want to use our daycare center because you know we have the best. And I love being the best. Oh, and you can always work from home for some things, but we can make it more as well. We are in the digital age after all, and I do not mind it. Hell, I'll come to your house. Especially, you know, for anything. I'm just so happy. I'm going to be an aunt." Paisley paled for a moment, and then I realize what had just happened.

Because Paisley meant aunt as in Devney's friend, not the ex-wife of her brother-in-law.

"Yes, you're going to be an aunt," Devney said, gripping Paisley's hand, and then mine. "Both of you are. Of course, I have more than a few brothers and sisters, so there's going to be plenty of aunts and uncles involved. I'm just so damn excited. We're going to have a baby. All of us. And thank you, Paisley. There wasn't one moment where I was worried about work, because I knew that, no matter what, we would find a way to make it work. Even if I had to take extra time off because I wasn't sure how long my maternity leave would go."

"Well, at least four to six months right? Screw that one month thing."

"I love you," Devney said with a laugh, and then the two of them were hugging, and I was standing back, feeling as though I'd been blindsided.

Because not once had Devney worried about work. Paisley had a healthy and welcoming business which knew that people procreated and that meant things would need to change. And Paisley would find a way to make that work.

And I knew that if my boss found out I was pregnant right now I wouldn't be fired, because that would be illegal, but I would lose out on that promotion and any thought of being able to work from home. I would lose prestigious clients, and I would be treated like the fragile lily he thought I was, rather than the fierce kick-ass Addison I fought so hard to be.

I would lose it all.

Why was I fighting so hard to keep it?

But before I could answer that terrible question, Devney gave me a look, her face falling.

"What's wrong? I'm sorry that I sort of took over this whole evening. I just really wanted to tell my friends. Heath is telling his brothers and sister tonight. You know, a whole family thing. And I wanted to do it with my part of the family. I'm telling my actual kin tomorrow. Are you okay, Addison?"

I opened my mouth to say something, to pretend and then tell them later, but instead I burst into tears.

Devney looked pained before she threw her arms around me, pulling me close.

"What's wrong? Oh my God."

I shook my head and wiped my tears, annoyed with myself, because Devney needed this happiness and I was ruining it. "I'm so sorry, Devney. I'm so happy for you. You're going to make an amazing mom. And yes you're going to have all 1,000 of us aunts and uncles by your side no matter what. I'm truly blessed to be your friend and to be part of this. I love you and I love this."

Devney was crying now too, but Paisley just

frowned at me. "Then why are you crying? What's wrong, Addison?"

I pressed my lips together, trying to gain the courage to say the words, and I knew that courage would never come so I just needed to get it out there.

"I had you guys over tonight because I was going to tell you I'm pregnant." I gave a brittle grin. "Surprise."

Paisley just blinked at me, while Devney dried her tears and frowned.

"You're pregnant? How? Who? What? Why?" Devney shook her head. "Wait, I've run out of questions, but what?"

Paisley pointed to Devney and then at me. "Yes, what she said. You're both pregnant? At the same time? Oh my God."

"Exactly, oh my God," Devney added, and I burst out laughing, feeling the ridiculousness of the situation. There were way too many emotions all at once.

"I'm pregnant. And I was trying to figure out how to tell you, but yes. I'm pregnant. About to start my second trimester."

"Oh my God, me too."

Devney blurted out her due date, and I nodded, my hands shaking.

"About a week after that."

"Oh my God, baby math is going to do me in,"

Paisley said, before she went to my fridge, and pulled out the bottle of wine that I'd had in there for a while.

"Since neither of you two bitches can drink, I'm going to be doing this. And then, Addison, I would love some answers to any of those questions. Yes, I realize you can keep them to yourself because I am the queen of privacy and not telling anybody what I feel, but please, let us know something."

She poured a very large glass of wine, and then drank half of it in nearly one gulp.

That was pretty impressive.

Devney still held my hand as Paisley looked between us, the wine glass still in her hand.

"So, do you remember your birthday party? And how I got really drunk, as did Luca?"

Devney's eyes widened as Paisley laughed and sipped more of her wine.

"Well, I'm pregnant. And it's Luca's. And we're going to keep it. And we're going to remain friends. And we're going to pretend that we didn't have sex again while at the retreat."

Devney's mouth dropped open wide, like a fish, as Paisley laughed and sipped more of her wine.

"You mean the trip where he pretended to be your fiancé? Oh. This is gold. These fucking Cassidy brothers just make you crazy. You are a sane, rational woman, Addison. And I am so damn happy for you."

For some reason I thought Paisley was going to admonish me, and I just stared at her.

"What?"

"You're having a baby. And you're keeping it. And you sound happy even underneath the fear. I have no idea what is going to happen next, and I'm here for it. Because you guys are my family too. I'm excited for you. I promise."

That made me cry again, and then Paisley and Devney were there and I was holding onto them both.

"I'm so sorry for stealing your thunder," I told Devney, who just laughed.

"I was about to tell you that I stole your thunder. What were the chances we were both going to tell each other tonight that we're pregnant?"

I shook my head. "I have no idea. I also have no idea what's going to happen with Luca, or how I'm going to handle work and being pregnant and being a mom, but we'll figure it out. Because one of the hurdles is over. I told my best friends. I'm having a baby."

My mouth went a little dry, and Paisley laughed again.

"You know, I was coming over here to tell everyone

that I had a boyfriend, but you know, I guess babies beat out boyfriends."

Devney and I looked at each other, before we blurted out at the same time, "Who, how, when?"

"Oh, I'll tell you about Jacob later, first though, let's talk babies. And Luca. Because wow. That's, that's going to be interesting."

And as I sat down eating mushrooms and lasagna with my friends, I knew interesting was one word for it.

I just didn't have any answers to the questions they asked.

And that was a damn problem.

Once they left, I made my way to Luca's, since we needed to talk. We had planned this earlier, as he'd wanted to make sure I was okay, and I knew I'd need to debrief.

I just hadn't expected that debriefing to go as wild as it had.

Boyfriends and babies, oh my.

Luca opened the door before I could even knock, and then I was in his arms, my head on his chest.

"Hey there. Are you okay?"

There was a dog with a cone around his neck in the corner and kittens mewing from their little kennel near the couch, and I just sighed at the craziness of it all.

"They know."

Luca nodded, running his hands down my back.

"I take it you know about Devney, too?"

I winced. "Yep. Did you tell your brothers?"

He nodded. "Yes and they didn't punch me. It's a big fucking news night. Are you okay?"

"I think so. Maybe. I don't know. Oh, and Paisley has a boyfriend."

Luca's brows rose. "That was not discussed tonight."

"I really don't know if I can deal with everyone else's problems right now, but okay. They know. There's no turning back."

"Baby, I don't think there ever was."

And because I was an idiot, because it just felt good in his arms, I went to my tiptoes and kissed him, and when he kissed me back, I knew we were in deep trouble.

Chapter Eleven

Luca

I had my hands in Addison's hair as she knelt in front of me, the bad idea between us just increasing with every taut breath.

"Are you sure this is what you want? I can stop."

She looked up at me, those doe eyes wide, and it was the sexiest damn thing I'd ever seen. She still had on that little dress she had worn, the cardigan she had put on over it when she first arrived was long gone. She'd stripped off my shirt the moment she kissed me, and somehow we were back in my bedroom, all thoughts of promising never to do this again firmly out the window. It felt so right, so why would it be wrong?

I was pretty sure there were a few songs about that. Ones that told me that I was making a mistake, but I didn't care.

All I cared about was her.

"Please? This is one thing we never got around to doing." And then her hands were on the button of my jeans, and I swallowed as she undid it and freed me.

My cock sprang out, hard and ready. I was always hard around her, even before our first kiss.

I had gotten good about ignoring it though, because it wasn't something that I was supposed to think about. *She* wasn't someone I was supposed to think about.

I didn't think there was any going back now.

"Be a good girl then, and suck my cock. I want you to swallow it whole. I want it to touch the back of your throat. Can you do that without gagging? Are you going to have to be very careful?"

"I guess you're just going to have to see if I have a gag reflex or not," she muttered before she took me in hand and I groaned, keeping my hand in her hair. She thought she was going to be the one that controlled this, but no, it was going to be me. Just like every other time we had been in bed.

It was the damn hottest thing ever, and she was going to get used to me.

Because I wasn't backing down.

She slid her hand up and down my cock, keeping me steady, as I slid my thumb along her cheekbone and over her plump lips.

Her mouth parted and I slid my thumb inside.

"Suck."

She did, her tongue twirling around the tip of my thumb. I slid it in and out, mimicking what I was about to do to her, and then I pushed forward, the tip of my dick pressing against her open mouth.

"Swallow."

She opened her mouth and I slid deep inside, one small thrust, and then another. She hummed along me, hollowing out her mouth as I pressed deep, reaching the back of her throat. She gagged slightly, and I pulled away, tugging on her hair.

"You okay, baby?"

She nodded, my cock still in her mouth, so I moved forward, loving the way she swallowed, taking me deeper.

I wrapped her hair around my fist and began to move again, this time faster. Her hands dug into my hips as she bobbed her head. I forced her to stay still, needing to control the action so I didn't hurt her as I went deeper. She hummed along me, her tongue going flat to take more of me as I kept moving, sliding my cock down her throat. She was so beautiful on her knees, my cock in her mouth, her eyes wide. When my balls tightened I pulled out, my cock sliding along her lips, leaving them puffy, wet, all mine.

"I want to come inside you, not down your throat. Can you handle that?"

I didn't give her time to answer, instead I pulled her up and crushed my mouth to hers, needing her.

My hands moved, pulling the dress over her head and tugging her panties to the side.

She was quickly on her back, legs around me as I tugged her bra down, but not completely off. That way her tits were pushed up and I could cup them, rolling her nipples between my fingertips before sucking hard. They pebbled, reddening into the colors of cherries.

I hovered over her, sliding my fingers in between her wet folds.

"You're already so wet for me. Do you want this cock? Do you want me?"

"Luca, please."

She panted out the words and I growled, sliding my cock against her lower lips. She was swollen, aching, and I pressed my thumb along her clit, rubbing small circles.

"You're so damn beautiful."

"I can't, I can't."

I leaned forward and slowly slid deep inside. She was tight, so tight I had to grind my back molars together so I could maintain some sense of control.

"I've got you," I whispered. "I've got you."

"Luca, I need you to move. Please."

I smiled against her mouth, loving this.

Loving the fact that this felt familiar and new all at the same time.

I kept kissing her as I slid in and out of her, slowly at first, and then faster.

I pressed her knees up to her shoulders, going deeper than before, and her eyes rolled to the back of her head, her chin lifting. I took that as permission as I kissed up and down her throat, biting gently on her shoulder.

When she started shaking, I played with her clit again and she came, her legs wrapping around my waist.

I moved then so I was sitting at the edge of the bed and she was straddled over me.

The movement pushed her face right against mine and I kissed her, needing her taste, just needing her.

Everything was happening so fast, and I knew if I wasn't careful I was going to fall. But was that so wrong?

I had fallen before, and had nearly broken, but I wouldn't let that happen again.

Not with her.

Not with Addison. My Addison.

I slid deep inside her again and let her rock her body over me, breathing into each other, leaning into each other.

And when she came for the second time, I followed, filling her, marking her as mine. I didn't care if it was ridiculous and annoying and growly and absurd.

I wanted her to be mine. I wanted to claim her and mark her and let everyone else in the world know that she was mine.

I was such a territorial jackass, and I didn't give a flying fuck.

Her body shook as we both came down from our orgasms. I smiled, running my hands up and down her back.

"You okay, baby?"

"I don't think I can move."

I grinned and kissed her gently before standing. She let out a small squeak, wrapping her legs around my waist as I carried her, still balls deep, to the shower.

"Luca, don't drop me."

"I'm not going to hurt you. Either of you."

The seriousness of the situation seemed to take hold, but we didn't say anything. I turned on the shower and blocked her from the cold water, needing the icy chill to help me calm down. It didn't matter that I had just come. I was still hard as a rock inside her.

Thankfully the water helped, and I set her down.

"Will you stay the night?" I asked as I lathered soap over each of us.

She took the loofah and washed me, the act gentle, far more intimate than we had been before.

"Okay. I'd like that."

I smiled at the admission before I kissed her again. When I laid her in bed, I just held her.

"We should stop doing that, you know."

I smiled, even though I knew she couldn't see me.

"You're right. It's very wrong."

"And probably going to be a huge mistake in the future."

"Totally." I kissed the top of her head. "But I don't regret it. I don't regret you, Addison."

Her grip on my waist tightened, before she relaxed.

"Same. Same."

And as I lay there with her in my arms, I finally relaxed.

Addison left early the next morning, since she hadn't brought a change of clothes. And I knew that she hadn't on purpose. Because if she even thought about a future such as that, this would become real for her. And while it was real for me, I knew that this was all way too much for her to accept in one go. So I wasn't going to make it an issue.

If I did, then I would lose her before I truly even had her.

I knew both of us well enough to know that.

"Where is your head?"

I looked up at Colt and laughed.

"I have no idea right now. What's up?"

"Nothing. Just wondering when you were going to hand me the paperwork that I needed. You doing okay, buddy?"

I shook my head. "I think so. Hell." Colt sighed and leaned against the doorway.

"You and I have been friends for what, a decade? Since you were a wee babe not even old enough to shave those tiny chin hairs, or even have pubes. Now you're a big boy and about to have a baby of your own. Times sure have changed."

I scowled at my friend.

"Are you serious right now? That's what you're leading with?"

"I'm just saying. We've been friends for a long time."

"You had to mention my pubes. I'll have you know they grew in."

"And I'm very proud of you. Go you and your pubes."

I knew that none of the staff were back here, and it was quiet in the morning at our office, but I still cringed.

"We should probably stop saying that before we get sued for harassment or something."

"You're probably right. However, you want to tell me what's going on with you? You've been acting crazy for a few weeks now. And while I appreciate that you finally told me that you and Addison are having a child together, I would love to have more information. Like, how long have you two been together? When did it start? How are things going?"

I ran my hands over my face, annoyed with myself for letting things get so crazy and entangled. But what else was I supposed to do? That was life.

"Colt..."

"Don't Colt me. I work far too many hours, just like you, and I suck at people. But we are friends, even if we don't hang out every weekend because we hang out and eat lunch together every single fucking day here. I just didn't realize how close you and Addison were getting. So talk to me. I'm in the mood to talk about feelings. This will never happen again."

I laughed, I couldn't help it. Because that was true. Colt did not like to talk about feelings, except maybe with his husband. And even then, I wasn't sure.

"My head is in the clouds right now, probably because I slept past my alarm."

"Because of your girlfriend staying the night at your house? A girlfriend I didn't know about?"

I laughed. "Your fishing is more like sending tiny little bombs into a lake and seeing what pops up. You know, what floats."

"Well, what's floating? I feel like I should say that to you from now on. What's floating, Cassidy? Tell me all the details. Before I quit caring about your feelings. Because I'm about to do that."

"I still don't know how you landed a catch like Dane."

"I'll have you know Dane loves me for who I am. Grouchy asshole and all."

"Well, I love you too. Just not like that."

"I know. I've never been on your radar. But that's fine, you weren't on mine. You were too young. Too innocent. And, you know, you had Ashleigh."

I had known Colt long enough that he and his husband Dane had met Ashleigh. And they both grieved with me when she died.

It seemed like forever ago that it had happened.

That I had lost my one and only girlfriend.

How the hell was that even possible? The one girl-friend I'd ever had, the only person I had ever been with before Addison, was Ashleigh. And she was gone in a blink of an eye and there was no taking that back.

There was no finding a way through that grief. Though I had somehow. And I knew moving away from Portland had helped.

Now I didn't know what I was supposed to do next.

"Losing Ashleigh was probably the hardest thing that's ever happened to me in my life, and that's a lot, considering my family."

Colt took the seat in front of me, and steepled his fingers in front of him.

"I know. I watched it happen. Your parents are a piece of work, and I always liked you and Ashleigh together. But you're not the kid that you were when you were with her, you know."

I frowned. "What do you mean?"

"Grief changes you. I saw it with my mom when dad died. She was a completely different person before his death, and then after. When she got married again? I thought I would hate the guy. But he made my mom smile. And it took a while for my mom to smile again, so I was happy to see it."

"I remember you telling me that, vaguely, when I

was trying to get through the grief."

"You don't get through it, you wade through it, you sink and you drown and then you find your way up to the surface again. And look at that, another floating metaphor." He winked, and this was the Colt that I loved. He was an asshole, but he got you. And once you were his friend, he never let you go. Even across states. "I'm glad to see you with Addison though. She makes you happy. Although, you look a little growly right now. So, why don't you tell me what's going on?"

I shook my head, aware that my brothers might know about the whole fake fiancé thing and the pregnancy, but they were so tied up in their own worlds, for good reasons, that I was afraid to tell them the truth. Because I didn't even know my own truth.

"I know I'm not that man anymore. And honestly, I'll always think of Ashleigh. Always wonder what we could have had. But I have been ready to move on for a while now."

"That's good. You're moving on with Addison and having a baby. That's goddamn amazing, man."

I smiled brightly, I couldn't help it. "I know right? I'm going to be a dad."

"Well, that's going to be one scary thing. We'll figure out the hours for the practice. We'll make it work. That's why it's just the two of us. Because we're not going to be corporate snobs that don't let men have time off for their kids or something. We'll find a way to make it work."

I grinned. "I never had any doubt."

"So. You and Addison. You're going to give me any details?"

"I don't know really what to say, other than we're trying to figure it out."

"Trying. So, you went all the way up to the mountains to help her and pretend to be her fiancé, and yet you're not even going to tell me if she's your girlfriend or not?"

I cringed. "I think I was better at pretending to be a fake fiancé than wondering if I'm a real boyfriend. Now isn't that a kick in the ass?"

"Excuse me?"

My eyes darted up at the open door that I had forgotten we hadn't closed, and all the blood drained from my face.

Because I knew that nasally voice. I had heard it a few times over that weekend.

Mrs. Harrington-Wells III.

I had never gotten her first name as she only went by her husband's, a.k.a. Addison's boss. And from the way the woman fumed, she knew. She had heard it all.

I'd just made a gigantic mistake that was going to ruin everything. Addison was going to kill me.

Chapter Twelve

Addison

I bent over and looked underneath the stall doors and sighed in relief when I realized it was empty. I wouldn't have long, but I didn't need long for what I wanted to look at.

Bracing myself, I turned sideways in the mirror and then lifted my bulky sweater over the top of my brown linen pants so I could see what I had been trying to hide that morning.

"How the hell did this happen overnight?" I asked myself and shook my head.

I was officially in my second trimester, and I had

popped out like a little Turkey thermometer on Thanksgiving.

I wasn't huge yet, but I could definitely tell that there was a baby bump there.

I had thankfully worn baggier clothes today, but it didn't feel like it was enough. My face was starting to change and my ankles were already swelling. I didn't know if that was because I was drinking too much water or not enough. The fact that I didn't know told me that maybe I should come to terms with the fact that this was changing everything, I would no longer be able to hide it.

I would have to tell my boss soon, and then figure out my next steps.

Because the pregnancy was real but the engagement wasn't, and no matter what happened with Luca and I in the future, we were still not ready for anything resembling a commitment like that.

I frowned and looked down at the ring I still wore; hadn't even thought twice about putting it on that morning. My fingers were a little swollen, but the ring was large enough that I still had room to move it around. I honestly hadn't thought about it. I slid on the ring that morning as if it were natural. Everyone here thought I was engaged, so I needed to keep the ring on.

At least, that was the excuse I kept telling myself.

I quickly adjusted my clothes in case anyone walked in, then made my way back to my office.

I stopped and talked to a few of my coworkers, answering questions and getting a few answers of my own, before heading back to my desk to work on my major client list.

I didn't know when they would tell us about the promotion, but I knew it would be coming any time now. Travis looked nervous, and I counted that as a win. I wanted this job. I needed it.

Only, sometimes it felt as if I were fighting constantly for what, to work longer hours?

Because no matter what, even if I was working from home, I would still work long hours, just like Nathan.

He and Kelly were going to be trying for a family soon, and I didn't know if he would even stay with the company. From the way he and Kelly talked, perhaps he would move on to something that was a little more flexible.

Or thoughtful.

"Hey, Lily, do you have client C's report?"

I nodded and looked up at one of the team members. "I do. It's in the file."

"I don't see it. Can you send it again?"

My temple started to throb, and I clicked two buttons on the keyboard, and nodded.

"Done. And I just confirmed it was in the folder."

"Are you sure? How do you refresh it?"

I didn't roll my eyes, I didn't growl, I just put on a pleasant smile. "You click the button that says refresh."

"Oh, well, thanks. I need to get that to the boss. Thanks for doing that. I don't know what we'd do without you. You're always so reliable."

The guy left and I frowned, wondering what the hell that meant.

Reliable? Is that why I was still here? Because I was reliable?

All I did these days was work my ass off, and then clean up after everyone else when they realized that they didn't know what they were doing.

Why was I still here?

Yes, this was the number one company in the city, or it had been. There were up-and-coming companies out there that needed what I did, and yet I wanted to be the best. I needed to be.

At least, that's what I always told myself.

But I was tired. Tired of lying and fighting and pretending that I didn't resent being here.

Maybe it was just the hormones, or I needed to eat.

I just wasn't quite sure where I saw myself here when the baby came.

I would legally get my time off for maternity leave,

but they didn't have an on-site daycare. So we'd have to find different childcare, and since Luca and I didn't live together, we'd have to figure out where our child would be living. How custody would work. How we would work. And if I was here all the time, how would I be a mother?

These weren't new questions, nor did I have any answers. These were things that women and men dealt with every day when they tried to balance work-life and home-life. I knew I wasn't special, but the fact that I didn't have answers to my own questions right now worried me.

"If you keep frowning you're going to need Botox between those eyebrows sooner than later."

I looked up at Travis and didn't roll my eyes, but it was a near thing. "Are you serious? That's the dig you're going with? Botox?"

"I'm just saying. You're probably going to need it soon. You know people get lines there because they frown so much."

"I'm not sure why you're even saying this at work."

"Because we both know you won't go to HR. You never do."

Because our HR representative was sleeping with one of the major partners, and we both knew that so there was no use saying it out loud.

This company was becoming so toxic, or maybe it always had been. Maybe I just thought I could fight my way to the top. But I was going to win. I was going to beat Travis.

"Harrington and I missed you out on the golf course this weekend."

My eye twitched, and I stood up, smiling at him, knowing he could probably see the hatred in my eyes.

"Really? Sucking up that much in order to try to get this promotion? We both know he'll see through that."

From the way Travis looked at me, I had a feeling neither of us believed that for a second.

"We had a squash game on Saturday morning, so don't worry, I didn't need to play golf too. He much prefers squash and pickleball."

Travis's jaw tightened, and I beamed.

"Something wrong?"

"Well, you can try to see if that would help, because we both know you can't play golf. Does it really matter? Though, I do find it odd that you're no longer using your body in order to get ahead. Are you trying to look like a woman dressed in a potato sack?"

"My clothing has no bearing on what I can do. I'm the best person for this job, and we both know it. I have the highest rated clients, and I bring in the most ROI. You don't stand a chance."

Travis leaned forward, hands in his pockets. "If we really thought it was about the money that you can touch, neither one of us would be fighting this hard, would we? How is dear Luca? I have to admit, I was surprised anyone would actually want to be with you. You were always so cold when we were together."

"Get out."

"Touched a nerve, did I? Well, at least something's being touched. Am I right?"

"You know, I don't care if HR does nothing, I'm still going to go and talk to them."

"Go for it. We both know that you're lying. There's no way you suddenly had a fiancé the moment I did."

"And I take it you're marrying Dory because you love her?"

"Dory is perfect for me. Classy, privileged, with high connections, and brilliant. Everything that you aren't. You were fun in college, babe, but there's nothing else for you now, is there?"

I did not know what I had ever seen in this man. Either he had been so good at camouflaging that I had missed all the red flags, or I'd had my head in the sand, trying to focus on everything other than what was right in front of me.

Travis was the first man I dated after discovering I had the clotting issue.

Travis had pretended to be supportive, though he never knew why I had been depressed.

He had swooped in because I had been an easy mark, and I hadn't seen it for what it was.

"I'm going to get the promotion, Lily. And then they're going to realize that you can't be the best at everything. You can't even be the best at a few things. But that's okay. You'll learn it eventually."

With that, Travis left. I watched him go, wondering once again why I had thought it would be a good idea to ever date him.

Being young and stupid was only good for so many excuses.

I went back to work, trying to focus, although I couldn't. Not with the promotion on the line, my stomach growling, and people coming in and out of my office all day to ask me for things.

Some things were in my purview, but others? I was slowly coming to realize that because I kept saying yes in order to get ahead, people used me as if I was their admin.

If I told them no, to do their work on their own, they gave me a weird look. That had always been the case though. I didn't do what people wanted me to do just because it would be easier for them, but I was tired.

Tired of this rat race.

And I had no idea what I was going to do about it.

"The boss is wanting us to come into his office soon. Just so you know."

I scowled at Travis. "Why are you back here?"

"I just wanted to say I hope the better man wins."

I rolled my eyes. "Not even subtle."

"What does being subtle have to do with it? I want to win."

My phone buzzed and I hit ignore after seeing Luca's name. I would call him back. I needed to deal with the man in front of me and the fact that the boss wanted to meet with us.

When Luca called again immediately, alarm hit me, but then the boss's admin was at the doorway.

"You're both requested in the office now. Put down what you're doing and come on."

I met Travis's gaze and smirked.

"I suppose time will tell. It is time, isn't it?"

"It's my time."

And then he turned, leaving me behind. I grabbed my phone, doing my best not to run after him.

My phone buzzed one more time, and I texted Luca without looking.

"Call you right back."

This was it. I would now know if my lies and my hard work had paid off.

If they hadn't? I wasn't sure what I would do. But I'd figure it out.

I always did.

But I usually always won.

When I walked into the office, Travis was already sitting in a chair with a wide grin on his face, and I wondered what I had missed in the ten seconds I had been behind them.

But then I realized the boss wasn't alone.

No, his wife stood behind him, one hand on his shoulder and a scowl on her face.

The blood drained from my face, as I looked at her, then to Travis, then at my boss's eyes.

Something had happened.

Something had gone really wrong.

"Take a seat, Addison. We need to talk."

Addison. Not Lily.

They knew, and I was about to get fired.

Fired from the job I wasn't even sure I wanted anymore.

And the fact I had even thought that when I had been doing my best not to think about it at all? That said enough.

"It's come to my attention that the integrity that we expect within these walls hasn't truly reached the level we've required. This is a company that strives itself on success, hard work, and truth."

My heart raced, bile coating my tongue.

"Mr. Wells—"

"No, I believe I will continue to talk. My wife has a puppy, you see. A gift from her brother." He waved the puppy off as if it didn't matter and everything started to click into place.

Puppy. Luca.

All his calls.

What the hell had happened?

"I went in to see the vet, a new one, because I met that Luca and he seemed very competent. But I was surprised to hear that the relationship I thought was so strong, such a wonderful asset to this company, was a lie." Mrs. Harrington-Wells clucked her tongue and I stiffened, needing to know how she figured it out, but afraid to ask.

"You lied to us. After we have put so much effort into you, you lied. It was already going to be neck and neck between you and Travis for the promotion, and you already had such a hard path in front of you, considering your background and how much Travis brings to us."

Anger flowed through me and I curled my hands into fists, ignoring the smirking man at my side.

"Excuse me? Travis and I come from the same schools, with the same connections. What path are you speaking of?" I asked.

My boss ignored me.

"You lied to us, and lying will not be tolerated. And while we won't let you go for that transgression, you have to know that you will be reprimanded. Travis will become our new junior partner. He's earned it. And his connections with the Forbes, as well as his hard work and determination will be an asset to this company. And Addison—Lily—you will have to work hard to get in our good graces again, but I'm sure you will. You've always worked your best."

Travis gloated as he said, "Thank you." I wasn't quite sure what they said after that, it sounded like echoes around me.

Why had I fought so hard and made so many poor decisions for a job that didn't respect me, one I wasn't even sure I liked anymore.

My entire five-year plan was gone, my ten-year plan? It was like it hadn't even existed.

I had made mistake after mistake, for people that didn't respect me. And never would.

"I quit."

I hadn't realized I was going to say the words until they were out, hadn't ever thought I would, but then they were there, and everyone stopped speaking and looked at me.

"Excuse me?" Harrington-Wells III asked as Travis chuckled beside me. He thought he was the victor, but I couldn't care less.

"I quit. I don't want to work here anymore. Not for you, not with him, not for a company that has never valued me. Yes, I lied. I made up a fiancé because I knew that if I showed up as a single woman I wasn't even going to be considered for the promotion."

Harrington held up both hands. "Excuse me, I would never condone harassment such as that. I've never thought less of you for being a woman."

This time I smirked. "We both know that's a lie. We both know that this is a boys' club and always has been. I'm your token woman, and I had thrived because I knew I could do better. I could be better. But I'm done. I lied because I knew if you found out the truth, you would've found a way to let me go anyway."

Then I stood up and shifted my shirt so they could see the bump.

Travis's eyes widened, as Wells's wife clucked her tongue once again, and my boss just paled.

"I'm done. I don't need this job. I don't need this business. And you're going to be sorry after I'm gone. You don't even have any idea how to open up a PDF, and the man you just promoted hasn't done his own work in months. But sure, reward the snark."

I stormed out of the office, blind panic setting in.

I had just made a colossal decision, one that I had been brewing over in the back of my mind for months.

And one that screamed I was making a giant mistake.

But there was no going back.

No changing anything.

They would've found a way to fire me. And now I needed to deal with the consequences of my actions.

And yet, I felt relieved.

Which should have scared me more than anything.

Chapter Thirteen

Luca

My pulse raced when Addison opened the door. I was ready to be murdered. That was pretty much what was about to happen. She was going to murder me, and it would be entirely justified.

"I messed up. I fucked up so bad. I'm so sorry."

Addison looked up at me with wide eyes and shook her head.

My stomach dropped and I let out a shaky breath. I deserved whatever was coming. Because I had been so stupid. All of our not-so-careful plans were now tossed up into the air, and nothing else mattered.

The moment that I had seen Mrs. Wells at my door, I had jumped up and tried to fix the situation, but the older woman had just held up her hand, clucked her tongue in that odd way that always annoyed the hell out of me, then left me alone, while Colt and I had tried to stop her. I had tried to reach Addison over and over again, but she hadn't responded. I just got a text back an hour later saying that I should come over.

Colt had taken my last appointment, and I drove like a bat out of hell to her house.

I had ruined everything.

I hadn't even realized that I could. That I had the power to take something so precious, so meaningful, and throw it out the window.

"I'm sorry. I'm so damn sorry. I didn't even know that she knew where I worked, or that she'd be in the back office. Colt and I were just talking about what happened, because we talk about our lives. Did he fire you? He better not have fired you. I'll fight. I'll do whatever it takes. You do not deserve to lose your job because I'm an idiot."

"It's fine. It's really fine."

I shook my head again. "It is not fine. I'm so sorry."

"Come inside. I'm making decaf coffee with really fun creamers."

"Baby."

She took my hand and pulled me inside, closing the door behind her.

"I quit my job. You didn't get me fired."

I froze in place, watching as she tried to tug my hand and pull me after her. She was so cute, trying to tug me away, but she couldn't do it because she was so tiny.

And yet, she had so much strength and perseverance.

And I had clearly lost my damn mind if I had just heard that correctly.

"Wait, what happened now?" I asked, confusion evident in my tone.

"Come and have some decaf coffee with me. I guess I could make you real coffee. You'd probably like that more. I can't really have caffeine right now. At least, not the amounts that I used to have with my old job. Because it's my old job now."

"Your voice is going really high-pitched. Tell me, how can I fix this?"

That's when I realized she was wearing yoga pants and a crop top with a shawl over it, and her baby bump poked out.

Because she was showing.

Showing our child.

The entire world crashed around me and I wanted to reach out, to press my hand against her belly just to feel it, and I realized that maybe now was not the appropriate time for that.

Addison poured me a cup of coffee, added whipped cream and caramel sauce, and handed it over.

"Cheers. It's decaf but has tons of sugar. It'll be okay. I promise. Everything will be okay."

"You say that, and yet you're pretty much shouting those words. What happened, Addison? Other than the fact that I ruined everything."

She took a sip of her drink, and I did the same, wiping whipped cream from my nose.

"You didn't ruin everything. You sort of just helped me get pushed in the right direction, because part of me has been thinking that I've been making a mistake for a little too long now."

"I'm confused."

"Honestly, so am I."

She took a deep breath, and then began to pace the kitchen, her hand going to the swell of her stomach.

I was not going to think about how attractive that was.

There was seriously something wrong with me, but then again, I always thought Addison was attractive. And that was just one of the many problems with us.

"I realized that I've been trying for a promotion at a job that I don't even know if I like anymore. I mean, I should have liked the job. It's what I've been working towards since college."

"Why don't you take a seat?"

She scowled at me. "I don't need to sit. I'm just pacing. Going belly first because apparently I'm showing now and that is starting to really settle in so let me panic first over this and then we'll deal with the next step, okay?"

I nodded in silence before standing up and getting her a glass of water. She smiled, took a sip, and then set the glass down.

She was going to balk at me taking care of her, but I'd find a way. Even if I had to be sneaky about it.

"I was a freshman in college and I knew I wanted to go into finance. I loved numbers and I loved trying to make things work. And everything just led to this moment where I knew what company I wanted to work with because they were the best, and I wanted to be the best. I was a gifted student. Of course, you know that, you graduated early and went to vet school before I was even out of college. I'm two years older than you. I'm basically a cougar."

I shook my head. "Baby, you're not a cougar. You're only two years older than me. That doesn't really make you an older woman."

"Excuse me, but math says so. I'm preying on you."

"Addison."

She threw her hands in the air. "I know I sound ridiculous now but I'm losing my fucking mind. I worked so hard for that promotion, I made you lie for me, and in the end it didn't matter."

"Because I ruined it."

She shook her head. "But you didn't. I was never going to get that job, you know. It was always going to be Travis because it's a boys' club. And they would've found a way to make it so HR wouldn't notice, because it's not like our HR even paid attention to anything anyway. But there would have always been reasons for me to never get ahead. I would always have worked twice as hard, and never had any time for a life. Because the one time I actually had a moment of life, we did this." She pointed to her belly. "And I don't regret that, because I'm somehow really excited for this and scared to death, even though I don't know what's going to happen. But I realized as my boss was reprimanding me and making sure I knew I was going to pay for lying, even though I was never going to get the promotion in the first place, that I couldn't do it anymore. I hadn't wanted to be there for a while and it took me too long to realize that."

"Then why were you trying so hard for the promotion?" I asked, knowing it was probably the wrong question.

"Because I want to be the best. Just like you are. Just like all of our friends. We are all overachievers. I wanted to prove that I could do it, even though I didn't like doing it anymore. I quit my job. So now I don't get unemployment or severance or anything. But it's okay, I have a plan."

I leaned forward, interested. "Okay, that's good."

She laughed, shaking her head. "Okay I lied. I don't have a plan. But I'm pregnant and I don't have medical insurance and I have no idea what I'm going to do."

"We could get married," I blurted, wondering if I had just lost my damn mind. But it did make sense. I had medical insurance, and getting married would give her medical insurance. It would probably help the whole "how are we going to raise this child together" question, though not really. I knew I was falling in love with Addison, and I had no idea how she felt about me. As it was, we had spent our entire "relationship" trying to get her this promotion so she would have time off for our child, and now that was all thrown out the window.

Nothing made sense anymore, and I had no idea

what to even say in this moment, so of course blurting out we could get married was the perfect solution.

In answer, Addison threw her head back and laughed.

I didn't know whether to be relieved or disappointed in my random and horribly timed indecent proposal.

"One fake thing at a time, but thank you." She shook her head, smiling at me. "This is absolutely ridiculous. I had a five- and ten-year plan, and now I have no plan. Everything has gone off the rails and nothing makes sense."

"You really didn't want to work there anymore? Even without my involvement or the baby?"

Addison reached out and gripped my hand, and I frowned down at where we connected. I didn't know when I had started to need her touch, to crave it, but that was something I was going to have to deal with at some point, I just didn't know when.

When would it all make sense?

"I haven't been happy in a long time. Between my hours at work, and life in general, I just haven't. I kept working for the next thing and then I realized that I was fighting for something that I didn't even want anymore. And yes, quitting my job was ridiculous and impulsive, and I should have stuck it out until I had a backup plan, but I didn't, and now I'm going to have to deal with the consequences."

"We will. I'll help. I'll do whatever I can."

My lips twitched, even as I held onto her hand for dear life. "I don't think you need my help at the vet clinic. I wouldn't be very good at anything there."

"You'd be okay at it," I said softly, "But no, you're right. I didn't mean at my job, but in general. I'm here. Whatever you need. We're in this together."

"I need to go job hunting, while pregnant. That isn't going to be easy."

"I could tell you what you already know, that it's illegal for them to discriminate against you for being pregnant. But we also know that it's not going to stop them from having their biases." My jaw tensed as I thought it, but in reality, there was nothing I could do but support her. Even if it killed me.

"It's only been a couple hours, and I know I'm still in panic mode. I don't know what I would have done outside of that, but I have to think this is for the best even as I freak out. Soon I'll actually start to want to throw up again, and that will have nothing to do with being pregnant. But I will find a job. I've always kept my resume current, because that was just something I always did. So, here we are. Try not to panic."

I stood up and leaned forward, cupping her face in my hands.

She froze like a deer in headlights and looked up at me. "Luca?"

"You hated that job. I'm happy you're gone. This might not be the best timing, but maybe it is perfect. You finding something new that works for you that you can thrive in should happen before the baby gets here. But no matter what, I'm going to be here, okay? I promise."

"I know. Is it weird that I trust you no matter what? That my best friends are going to be there even though I pretty much threw everything out the window today?"

"I've got you. Always."

I wanted to lean down and brush my lips against hers and hold her close so she knew everything would be okay.

But the doorbell rang and I let my hands drop, willing myself to breathe normally. I wanted to hold her and protect her and take care of everything. Only that wasn't my job. If I was more of a growly asshole I would just make it happen, but that wasn't me.

I was the laid-back guy. The guy who hid what he was feeling because it was better just to go with the flow. It was what I was good at.

And that guy was in love with Addison. That guy was monumentally screwed.

"I don't know who that is, but my group chat has been wild since I told them I quit my job without any explanation."

I raised a brow. "You told the girls you quit your job in a text?"

"They were working because, you know, it was the middle of the day. I didn't want to bother them." Her eyes widened. "And you left your job in the middle of the day."

"And it's okay, I'm the boss, I can do that. I had someone cover for me and I'll handle all the paperwork later. It's in my car."

Someone rang the doorbell again and Addison moved past me to open it.

This had truly thrown a wrench in all of our plans, not that we had actually had any, so maybe starting from the bare bottom would help. Of course, I knew that once Addison finished her shock-panicking, things were going to get hairy.

She opened the door to find Paisley standing there with a box of cookies in her hand.

"Oh good, you're both here. That actually makes things easier. Congratulations, Daddy."

I opened my mouth to say something as Addison burst out laughing, tugging Paisley inside. "The absurdity of the situation is ridiculous. Did you bring me cookies? Oh, I like cookies."

Addison took the box from Paisley without saying anything else and moved to the kitchen island before proceeding to open the box and look inside.

Paisley met my gaze and I saw the worry there.

I shrugged, at a loss for what to do. Because this wasn't the Addison that I knew. The Addison I knew was self-assured and strong, this one seemed as if she were so lost that there was no way of getting out of it. We'd find a way, but I wasn't sure how.

"Paisley," I started, but she interrupted me with a smile. She really was beautiful, and I saw what my brother had seen in her, but I still didn't know her. She could be so closed off at times that it was hard for me to get a read on her.

"It's okay," she mouthed, before walking over to Addison. "So, now that you're done working for that asshole and his stupid company, you can work for me."

I grinned, because Paisley was a brilliant, brilliant woman.

Addison looked at her, then at me. "I'm sorry, what? Luca, did you tell her that she should hire me? Because you don't need to fix things for me. I don't like it when people try to do that."

I held up both hands. "I had nothing to do with this, though I do think it's a good idea."

"You haven't even heard the idea," Paisley said, before she grinned. "But it's a good idea. Work for me. Devney already does."

"You can't just hire me because I'm your friend."

"Actually, I can do exactly that. I'm the boss. You need a job, and I need someone with your talent for my multimillion-dollar company. I mean, I was going to try to poach you before, and then you went full speed ahead with this promotion thing, and now the pregnancy? It felt a little wrong to try and poach you. But now I don't even have to. You can come to me willingly. Look I'm the spider and you're the precious little fly in my web." Paisley frowned. "Not that, well, I shouldn't really call you a fly. I'm not going to keep you for later then eat you. At least parts of you. I really don't know how a spider eats a fly. I should look that up."

Addison set down her cookie, looking a little green. "And on that note, I'm done with the cookies."

"I think I'm done with anything remotely connected to food," I said, equally as queasy.

"I went off on a tangent, but for real. You're brilliant. And I was going to offer you a job. But I was going to be casual and cool and find a way to secretly make it happen so you wanted to work for me. You could work for anyone in this town, or in any state for that matter."

Panic settled in, before Paisley looked at me. "Not that she's going to move. I mean, you're going to have a baby together. And your practice is here, you just moved here—and I'm going off into another tangent again. Anyway, you should work with us. I haven't told Devney I'm asking, but she and I have been talking about how amazing it would be to have you working with us. Because we would be able to take on the world. Between my departments, her in PR, and you coming in on finance? It's perfect. I've needed someone with your talents for a while now, and I haven't found them. Harrington-Wells III's loss is my gain."

"But I quit, he didn't fire me," Addison said as she wiped away tears. I cursed under my breath and handed her the box of tissues.

She mouthed the words "thank you" before taking one and blowing her nose.

"He was going to make sure you never got what you deserved anyway. You deserve everything. And you should also know that now that I'm working with Kelly, I'm trying to also lure Nathan over. But you guys would be in two separate positions so it won't be a competition thing. I want the best, and you are the best. You can work from home, you can arrange things however you need to. And with Devney also pregnant, I already said that I'd be working on expanding the childcare section, so there you go. We'll find a way to make it work. Because I believe that no matter how you choose to live your personal life, my company shouldn't be taking the life out of you. Work for me. Get medical insurance, get that paycheck, and get a job that you could actually do with joy. Make me happy. Because it is all about me."

I needed Addison to say yes. Because just the thought of her moving to work for a better company in another city? That hadn't even occurred to me. I'd been so worried about making sure that Addison didn't panic that I didn't think about the fact that she could leave. She could go at any time, and we still didn't even have a plan. I hadn't even told her how I felt. I had barely let myself think about what I felt.

Because I was in love with her. At least, that's what I thought this feeling was. I hadn't really had it like this before. It had been different with Ashleigh. Everything had been different with Ashleigh. But Addison wasn't Ashleigh.

I knew that, and so did she.

And now I was going in circles.

"Paisley, I can't be a pity hire."

"If you call yourself that one more time, I'm going to

hit you. And I don't want to hit a pregnant woman, but I will."

"I'm just...I don't know what to do."

"Work for me. Let me help with that part. You've got a lot on your plate." Paisley looked between us, and finally Addison smiled.

"Okay. Okay."

She moved forward, presumably to hug Paisley, but before she took more than a step, she looked at me, her eyes wide with what looked like fear.

"I don't—" but she didn't get the rest of the sentence out before her knees gave out, and I ran towards her with my arms outstretched.

She fell into my arms, unconscious, and my world shattered.

"I should be back there with her. Why aren't I?" I growled, pacing the waiting room.

"Because you're not on her emergency contact list. Only her parents are, her parents who are out of town right now. But it's okay, she's going to let you back there, and everything is going to be okay."

I looked over at Paisley and raised my brow at her voice going that high-pitched.

"I see you're panicking with me right now?"

"All the damn panic. But it's okay. Everyone will get here soon and we're going to fill this waiting room, and then we're just going to find out that I gave her too much sugar with all those cookies and it's all my fault."

I held out my arms and Paisley reluctantly came into them, hugging me tightly for one moment before letting go.

"Thank you. I needed that. Please don't tell your brother."

My lips lifted into a smile despite the fact I had no desire to. "Don't worry, I won't. Did you call Jacob?" I asked, speaking of her boyfriend.

She nodded. "Yes, he's at work. He wants an update though."

"So would I."

"Luca Cassidy?" a big man in scrubs asked and I rushed over, my pulse racing. "Is she okay?"

"Addison would like to see you now. She's waiting with the doctor, so if you could follow me?"

I looked over my shoulder. "Let the others know?"

"Keep me updated," Paisley said, holding out her phone. I nodded and followed the large nurse to a room in the back.

Seeing Addison pass out like that had scared me to death.

She woke up not long afterwards, but I hadn't listened to her protests that she was fine. I drove like a bat out of hell to the emergency room, and since it was attached to the same hospital where her doctor saw patients, I counted that as fate.

But I hadn't been able to go back with her because I wasn't family.

I wasn't even technically her boyfriend.

She still wore my ring on her finger, fake as it was, but I was nothing to her.

Just the father of her unborn child.

"Here she is," the man said, and I nodded in thanks before stepping into the room and gripping Addison's outstretched hand.

She wore a hospital gown and her hair was piled on the top of her head. She looked fine, though she had an IV in her arm.

"What's wrong?"

"Everything's okay. Everything's okay."

Her doctor cleared his throat and looked at me. "Luca Cassidy?"

"Yes. I'm...I'm her...I'm the baby's father."

I held back a wince at that, though there wasn't any other way to say it. I didn't have words.

I didn't have a title.

"As I was just telling Addison here, her blood sugar

was low which was why she passed out. Everything is fine right now."

Relief slammed through me, until I registered the words *right now*. "But things could be wrong in the future?" I asked, frowning at Addison.

"Remember how I said I have a blood clotting issue? It's why I couldn't be on birth control."

"Are you okay?"

"I'm fine. I'm okay."

"But she's going to have to remain calm. I'm not putting her on full bed rest, but we will be taking precautions. For the next two trimesters, we're going to treat this as a high-risk pregnancy. So, let's go over what needs to happen."

The doctor started saying things, and I knew he was saying words, and Addison was taking notes, but all I could focus on was holding her free hand.

I couldn't lose her.

This couldn't be happening again.

Only it was.

And there was nothing I could do.

Chapter Fourteen

Luca

"You're going to what?"

I turned to Heath. "I'm moving in with Addison."

I was doing my best not to freak out even though it felt like that was all I was doing, and centering my own freakout was not going to help Addison.

Because if she wasn't calm, she could lose the baby. She could die. And I would not be the cause of that. I would do whatever it took to make sure she was healthy and didn't need to lift a finger.

"You're moving in with Addison? Does she know that?" August asked as he handed me my toiletry bag.

"Thank you. And yes. We already talked about it. Well, I sort of said I'm moving in and she's just going to have to deal with it, and she didn't argue."

"Because she's dealing with a lot right now," Heath put in, handing me my stack of jeans.

Considering my brothers didn't understand and thought I should probably not do this, they were sure being accommodating about helping me pack.

"She needs help. She's not on strict bed rest, but she's being forced to be stuck in her recliner or in bed while she's working, or even while she is in the house. She can be on her feet to take care of herself, but only for a certain amount of time each day."

"And you're what, going to take time off work?"

"No. I'm going to, I don't know. I can't be there twenty-four hours a day, but I can be there for some of it. When I'm not at the clinic making sure that my business doesn't fail, I'll be at her house. I don't see what the problem is. You would do that for any one of your friends."

"Addison isn't our pregnant friend. You know, you're going to be a dad, Luca. Have you actually sat down to think about this?" August asked.

"Of course I have. And I've no idea how we're going

to function after this. But it's one thing after another and I need to focus on this. So you know what I'm going to do? I'm going to make sure Addison has everything she needs. Her quitting her job now was probably the best timing because now Paisley is here saving the day."

"Paisley's good like that. She's making it so Addison can start her new job from home, right?" August asked.

"Yes. Thank God. And I know Devney and Paisley have a plan of their own, and Addison isn't happy with what's going on, nor does she have a plan beyond just making sure we don't screw things up. She can't do everything on her own, and I'm going to be there. Because she's my friend. Because she's having my kid, because I love her."

"There it is," August grumbled, pacing my bedroom.

"You're just going to blurt it out like that as if we were supposed to know all along?"

"What am I supposed to say? I didn't mean for it to happen. I did my best not to want her before all of this happened. I did my fucking best to let her just be my friend. But then I kissed her, and we did more than kiss, and I can't stop wanting her. I love her. But I don't know how she feels about me and it's not like there's been a good time for me to ask."

"Maybe before you offered to move in?" August asked, and I flipped him off.

"All I know is that I have to take care of her. Even if she never wants to be with me, even if we screw up whatever relationship we have and we're just awkward co-parents, I'm not letting her do this alone."

"You're a good man, you know," Heath said gently.

"I sure as hell don't feel like it."

"You know I hate talking about feelings, but do you want to talk?" August asked, and I pinched the bridge of my nose.

"I don't know what more there is to say. I love her. But I feel like that's not really high on the ladder of importance right now."

"I'm pretty sure you're wrong about that," Heath said.

"She knows about Ashleigh, right?" August asked, and I threw my hands up in the air.

"Yes. We all know about Ashleigh. And yes I'm panicking because the thought of losing Addison too? I won't do well, but that's not because of Ashleigh. Yes, the only other person I've ever loved died. And I can't get those times back. I can't get that feeling back. She isn't here and there's no fixing it. I grieved and I cried and I left the situation. I pretended that I knew what the hell I was doing all this time just so I could live. Because you don't get to pause time and grieve and find out who you are after someone that you love is gone. You have to look out into the future and pretend. You put on this mask so the world doesn't know you're dying inside. And I did a decent job of it. Yet even under that mask I figured it out."

"Figured what out?" Heath asked, his voice soft.

"That I'm always going to miss her. That I'm going to hate what happened until the end of my days. But also that I needed to learn who I am without her."

"I wasn't thinking that you were conflating Addison and Ashleigh in your mind, I was just being a guy worried about your feelings. I don't like being that guy." August rubbed his temples. "I'm really sorry. About all of this. And I am worried about Addison, just like you, but I'm also worried about my brother. Are you okay?"

"No. Of course I'm not. But Addison needs me to be strong, so I will be. I'm going to move in and make sure she's safe and healthy and has what she needs, and we'll take it from there."

"Taking it from there means you're going to be a father, Luca."

"You're going to be a father too, Heath." I grinned, I couldn't help it. "And even in all this insanity, we're going to be dads at the same time. How fucking amazing is that?"

"It's pure insanity, and I'm nervous. There're classes and books to read and I feel like I'm behind."

"I'm reading all that I can, and it doesn't matter that I have a so-called genius level IQ, I'm such a dumbass sometimes."

"Oh good, we can do this together."

"I love this bonding," August said dryly. "And since I'm the only one not currently impregnating the women in their lives, I'm just going to put it out there that if you need me, I'm here. I have weekends off when I know you don't always, so if the girls can't figure out a schedule so Addison doesn't get bored or stressed out or have a panic attack, I guess I could help."

I just stared at my brother, confused. "Really? You?"

"Don't sound so surprised. I have emotional growth. Sometimes."

"You're a good brother, you know."

"I try. Just don't get hurt, okay? I love you, you know. You're a dumbass but I love you. Addison has you and her support group, but she has us too. She's carrying my niece or nephew."

I smiled, then wrapped my arms around him, giving him a tight hug, doing the same to Heath.

I zipped up my bag and made my way to the front door, ready to head to Addison's.

The doorbell rang right as I got there though and I frowned in confusion.

"Who the hell's that?" I asked and opened the door without looking to see who was there.

I really, really should have.

Or maybe left a little earlier than this.

Our parents stood on the porch, not touching, not looking at one another. It was a familiar tableau.

Our parents were either all over each other and ready to show the world that they deserved to be together, or they were passive-aggressive assholes who hated one another and used that to become blockades between their children.

There was never any middle ground with them.

And from the tight look in my mother's eyes, and the set line of my dad's jaw, this wasn't going to be one of the good times.

"Mom, Dad. I wasn't aware you guys were in town."

"Your mother and I wanted to tell you something first, that way you can tell your brothers and sister. You were always the more rational one."

"Well, that's good to know," Heath said from behind me, his voice flat.

August didn't say anything, but I could feel the anger radiating off him.

My parents stilled, looking at each other then back at me.

"I didn't realize your brothers were here."

"Their cars are out front. Good job with the situational awareness. And I don't know why you think I'm the more rational one that's going to help with whatever the hell is going on between the two of you."

They finally noticed the bag in my hand.

"I didn't realize you were heading out," Mom said. "We'll be quick."

"Don't bother," August growled. "Just go."

"Don't talk to your mother with that tone," Dad snapped.

"Don't defend me," Mom reacted.

This couldn't be happening. Not again.

But as they bickered on my front porch, I realized of course it was happening again. These were the parents that had raised us, albeit reluctantly and not consistently.

"So, are you splitting up or getting divorced? Or are you trying an open marriage this time?" I asked.

"What?" my mom asked.

"If you're here to tell me that you guys are getting a divorce—one, I'm not surprised; two, I don't care. I have things to do."

"Please just let us come in, we have a lot to talk about."

"I can't. I have to go help the future mother of my child. Oh yes, you're going to be grandparents. I'm going to be a dad. Shocking I know. I know I'm not going to screw up my kid's life like you continually try to ours. And you are not going to even come near my kid when you're acting like this. You don't get to be those kind of grandparents."

I pushed through them and August began a slow clap, while I could hear Heath grumble under his breath.

"Grandparents!" my mom called out.

"We're too young for that. Who's the girl that you got in trouble?" my dad asked, and I whirled.

"You just assume I got a girl in trouble. Are you serious right now?"

"I'm just, I always thought it would be you and Ashleigh," my mom said, her eyes filling with tears.

I ignored the blow, because my parents were so selfish that nothing they said mattered. "Ashleigh's been gone a long time, Mom. You would know that if you had any concept of time when it has to do with human beings other than yourself."

"Why are you so mean to me?" Mom asked, honestly confused.

"I'm not being mean, I just don't want you here. Good luck on your divorce or whatever the hell is going on between the two of you. I don't care anymore. You've ruined my relationship with my sister and my brothers.

You forced me into the position I was in when I was younger when it came to school, and I fought my way out of that. You're not ruining the rest of my future."

"But we need you," Mom said, and I just turned and walked to my car, knowing my brothers would lock up.

I did not want to leave my brothers to deal with all of that, and I knew we'd have to talk to Greer soon, as our sister needed to know as well.

Why couldn't they make it work? I knew they loved each other, but they fought so often that it didn't make sense why they even tried to be together.

They just needed to make a final decision.

And as I pulled away and drove towards Addison's house, I wondered why I was putting myself into this situation.

I was nothing like my parents. I knew that. My relationship with Addison was nothing like theirs.

And yet for some reason all I could think about was the fact that if this didn't work out, if Addison and I couldn't figure our relationship out, I could hurt my kid just like my parents had hurt us.

And I didn't want that.

I pulled into her driveway slightly calmer to see the family text chat blowing up.

My brothers and Greer were all growling at one another, and I knew I would probably get yelled at by

August for leaving him alone with them. But I didn't care. Heath could handle it.

That's what big brothers were for.

I typed in the code to the door for Addison's house and walked inside, letting out a breath and telling myself that I could handle this.

We would handle this.

Addison lay in her armchair, a blanket over her lap with a baby book in one hand and her laptop to the side.

She was so damn beautiful. And she was mine. If I could get the balls to actually tell her.

"Hey," she said, her eyes a little sad. "Are you okay? Devney just said that your parents showed up at your house. Are they really getting a divorce again? I'm so sorry, Luca."

I set my bag down and moved towards her. I didn't even think about what I was doing before I was cupping her face and kissing her softly.

She hummed and pulled back, giving me that same sad smile.

"Luca?"

"I'm moving in, you know that, right? To take care of you and our baby. I'm not going to be my parents. I'm not going to split our time with this kid and screw them up and make our kid wary of us being in their life. I don't want to one day show up on my kid's porch and have them resent it."

Addison reached up and cupped my cheek and I leaned into the touch.

I loved when she reached out to touch me.

"Of course. No matter what happens with us, we're never going to be your parents. I hear enough of it from Devney. Don't worry. And yes, we already talked about you moving in. Because I really want to just relax and not have to lift a finger."

I took her hand in mine and kissed her fingertips.

"You never have to lift a finger. I've got them for you."

"This isn't going to be easy. It'll be months of me being stressed out and hormonal and not being able to do what I want. Of me learning a new job and having to do it remote. It's going to be baby books and doctor's appointments and life."

"I am going to be here for all of it. I work long hours, but I'm also the boss. And Colt and I were talking about adding on a new tech and an additional vet to help."

"That's not going to hurt the business?"

"No. We've just been lazy. Or unable to give up control."

"Are you going to have animals in the house?" Addison asked, then winced. "Not that pets are bad, I love them. It's just before I wasn't able to really be home enough to have any."

"Maybe overnights, like I have at my house. If that's okay with you? Hell, I didn't really think about that."

"No, that's fine. We'll make it work. Because you're here to help and I like spending time with you." She blushed as she said it, and it was as if someone had warmed me from the inside out.

I wanted to open my mouth and say something, to say that I loved her or cared for her, but nothing felt right, so I just leaned forward and took her lips again.

"I'm going to take care of you. Promise."

She searched my face and nodded at whatever she saw there, and a sense of relief slammed into me.

"I know you will. But just know I'm going to be a horrible bitch about this because I like taking care of myself."

I rolled my eyes. "Shocking. You, a bitch? I would never have guessed."

"You're very lucky that I'm not supposed to get out of this chair right now or I would beat the shit out of you."

"You could try. Now, I'm going to make some dinner."

"Paisley and Devney already put a few covered dishes in the freezer."

"Of course, but I'm going to make something from scratch just because it's my first night here." I winked. "And that means you have to eat whatever I give you."

"I feel like there's a dirty joke in there."

"Probably having something to do with a penis, but don't worry, I know you're not allowed to do that either." I let out a put-upon sigh, and she laughed.

"Sorry. This whole bedrest thing really sucks."

"Very much. But I'm going to be here the whole time, I promise."

I looked down at her hand and realized she still wore the ring. What was supposed to be fake was becoming all too real.

And I didn't mind it.

Only I was worried what would happen when she took the ring off, and living together for months set in.

That would be the true test of whatever relationship this was.

But I would make it work.

Even if it broke both of us in the end.

Chapter Fifteen

Addison

Months.

It had been months of me sleeping in this stupid armchair, or in my bed with pillows propped behind me, pretending that I wasn't going out of my mind.

Months of bed rest, and it was almost over.

Only two more weeks and this baby would come, and my life would change again.

Our life would change.

Sitting in my La-Z-Boy, I ran my hands over my swollen stomach, smiling as the baby kicked. I was only smiling now because the baby was kicking my hands and not my bladder. We had decided not to find out the sex of the baby, because we wanted to be surprised, as everything with this pregnancy and my current life situation was a surprise. It wasn't all bad, wasn't all scary, some of it was even good. Some of it was even surprising.

The baby was kicking, and everything was going well, and we were somehow making it work.

Luca was in the nursery, working on the finishing touches putting the changing station together. I had wanted to help, but had been scowled at when I offered, so I had sat in the rocking chair in the corner, pointing to where I wanted things, even though I changed my mind four times. This part of nesting hadn't been in the book. These hormones were making me insane.

I had been relegated to the living room armchair again, my feet up, as I read over a few more reports, taking notes for Paisley.

My friends and family were a godsend.

I knew I wouldn't have been able to make it through these months without them.

My parents were here often, helping with grocery shopping and helping me make sure that I was as ready for this baby as possible.

They hadn't even blinked an eye when they realized

that Luca wasn't sleeping in the guest room turned nursery, but was sleeping right beside me.

Luca and I hadn't even talked about it. The first night he moved in we had been lying on the bed, talking with one another about what we needed to do the next morning and for the rest of the week, when we had just fallen asleep mid-sentence.

Luckily he had set an alarm so he could head to work, but he hadn't left my bed since.

While it wasn't like the two of us could actually do anything with this heat between us, it was still there, even when I was grumbling about retaining water, that I felt disgusting, and just wanted to get out of this damn house, we still just clicked.

Because he was my best friend. Just like Devney was, just like Paisley was. We weren't in elementary school where the person you shared your glue stick was your only best friend. You were allowed to have more than one. Which had surprised me as an adult, but I was grateful for it.

"Okay, baby socks are all folded, and I know that as soon as we pull one out, the whole drawer's going to fall on the ground and we're just going to have to deal with it at two in the morning," Luca grumbled, and I smiled at him.

"I see my bad mood has moved to you."

Luca sighed and ran his hand through his messy hair, and I bit my lip.

I had been so horny these past few weeks. Hell, I'd been horny this entire pregnancy, and I hadn't been able to do anything about it.

Could you blame me?

Luca was gorgeous. He was only wearing gray sweatpants, and I had no idea where his shirt had gone and I did not mind. The man somehow had an eight-pack, and I knew it probably had to do with the fact that when he wasn't helping me around the house or working, he was working out.

Somehow he'd even gotten more muscular, even sexier, and I wanted to run my tongue all up against those abs.

"Stop staring at me like that," he grumbled.

"I can't help it. Go put on a shirt." My gaze went down to those gray sweatpants and the VPL there. "And maybe some underwear."

"I'm doing laundry, and I'm not in the mood to dirty more clothes. And if you like the look of my dick, keep looking. But you don't get to touch it. Apparently only me and my calloused palm get to touch it."

I snorted. "Oh, jerking off in the shower isn't to your liking anymore?"

"I'm so glad that I'm renting out my apartment on a

short-term lease right now, because if I wasn't, we wouldn't be able to afford the water bill."

"I told you you're welcome to jerk off right next to me. I wouldn't mind watching." I fluttered my eyelashes at him, and he flipped me off.

"Nope. It makes it worse. Because then you get all horny, and then you get sad, and then we have to just deal with it. Plus, I don't know, I just don't really want to jerk off sitting next to you while you can't do anything about it. Seems mean."

"It's very cruel. Will you help me up?" I asked, holding out my hands. "Uppies."

"Do not say that," he said with a laugh, as he helped me to my feet.

I was allowed to stand for a few minutes a day, and Luca timed those minutes when he was home.

And if he wasn't here, Paisley or Devney or my mother was. Heath had even shown up during the day because he worked afternoons and evenings, and August had shown up a few times, growled at me over the weekends, and I just learned to accept it.

He was going to be an uncle, he was part of this family. I was part of this family, even though Luca and I hadn't actually talked about what that meant.

We had talked about everything else. Bank accounts and breastfeeding and Lamaze classes and birth plans and house repairs and colors for the nursery. We had talked about so many things, but not actually about what would happen to us once the baby was born.

It was as if we were both afraid once we did talk about it, everything would change.

And that was the truth, but maybe it wouldn't change for the worse.

Or maybe I was just hoping for the best.

I didn't have a great track record knowing what I wanted, but I was learning.

At least I was pretending to learn.

"I really want some bubble water."

"Are you allowed to have bubble water?"

"Do not take away my bubble water, you've taken away everything else," I snapped. Then I cringed and gripped his hand. "I'm sorry. I'm just really excited for this baby to get out."

I wore a half sweatshirt that I had cut up into pieces over a tank top that showed most of my belly because I hadn't felt like changing, as well as a pair of his sweatpants.

They were dark blue, not the sexy gray kind, but they made me feel better. I had rolled up the bottoms because the man was a giant, but I felt gross and disgusting.

"We'll get you your water, go sit down."

"Just let me walk."

"Okay. I've got you."

We fell into our routine of him getting me water and a snack, because I was always hungry, and me getting things that I was allowed to reach.

We didn't even talk about what we needed from each other; it was just routine now. Like he had always been here.

And I liked it.

Maybe a little too much.

"So, how did that presentation with Paisley go?" he asked as he forced me to sit down again. I knew I needed to, but I didn't like being forced to do it. I was petty.

"Really good. She is such a godsend. I mean, I knew Paisley was brilliant because she's my friend and I only like brilliant people."

"You really are the mastermind behind all of this. And thank you for calling me brilliant."

"Okay gifted child who skipped grades and started college early. We already know you're brilliant. And I'm really excited to have those genes in this baby. But we're not going to force our child to start high school when he or she's a preteen, okay?"

"No problem. There's no way I'm going to force our child down the path my parents forced me. You know they only did that because they wanted me out of their way. They were busy with Heath being sick and then August always had sports and other things, they didn't know what to do with me. So they just pushed me into random classes."

"They pushed you yes, but you were also brilliant."

"Were?"

"I have baby brain. Leave me alone."

He leaned forward and kissed me on the lips, a casual kiss that could mean nothing or everything. I didn't shy away. We didn't freeze in the action as if it was too much, because it was just something we did now.

We had fallen into this relationship, and I liked it.

I felt like this was family.

And I loved him.

"Okay, Paisley?" he asked, pulling me out of my thoughts and revelations. Which was probably a good thing. Maybe.

"Well, I kicked ass, and the client is happy. And that also means Nathan can come and take over some of my work, as well as two other staff members, so that way they're not overwhelmed while I'm on maternity leave."

Luca shook his head. "I cannot believe that you and Nathan both left that company."

"It's a good thing we did since the company's being restructured."

The company I had worked so hard to strive for, and to become the best at, was no longer the best.

Apparently the way that Travis had become the "master of his craft" was through insider trading. He was gone, Harrington-Wells III was gone, having been fired by the board since Travis wasn't the only one who had been caught with his hand in the cookie jar. The head of HR who never listened to us was also fired. As was the person he had been sleeping with.

All in all, the company was floundering and the board had asked me to come back, as they did Nathan. They even called with a very nice package with a brilliant retirement plan, stock options, and so much more.

Saying no to them had been one of the greatest thrills of my life, something I hadn't even realized that I had craved.

And Nathan said no as well, and he and Kelly were expecting their first child later this year.

Somehow I had made a work family that actually wanted each other to succeed. And we were succeeding.

It was pretty damn amazing.

"Well, I'm proud of you. I knew you were going to kick ass. Are you excited to take some time off though?"

"Yes and no. I mean, we are going to have a baby." I did my jazz hands routine, and Luca laughed.

"Okay, that was stupid to say, but once you're done

with maternity leave, are you going to continue to work remote?"

I shook my head. "I don't think so, but I'll have the option. And there's a full daycare center now within the company; Paisley works fast."

"Damn straight. I'm just glad I didn't have to add a daycare next to the puppy kennel."

He winked as he said it and I rolled my eyes. "I'm just shocked that we don't have a litter of kittens here right now. You got them all homes?" I asked.

It was kitten season, which meant that we constantly had newborn kittens in the house that we were bottle feeding. It was good practice for the baby, but I knew that was going to have to stop once the baby came.

"Colt and our new team members that we hired are all handling it. We are on break from at-home visits with animals for a while until we find our routine. Everybody needs to be vaccinated and ready emotionally before I bring more animals home."

"You're a good person, Luca."

"I try. Although I will say, even though I haven't done it in a while, maybe an actual family member on four legs would be nice." He smiled at me brightly, and I narrowed my gaze. "You know, one that we don't have to give back to its owners or find a new family for. An old dog or cat that needs a home. A little kitten that can grow up with his brother or sister."

He dipped a piece of cucumber in ranch and stuffed it in my mouth before I could say no, and I chewed, annoyed that he knew exactly what I had been craving without me even saying it.

Damn that man.

"I know, I know, a vet without an animal at home does seem a little weird."

"It really does. The only reason I hadn't done it before was because I was constantly having animals at home, but now that we have the new center and our new team members, I don't know, I'd like to have a pet. However, baby comes first."

"That is very true."

My phone buzzed and I looked down at it, seeing my mom's name on the screen.

Mom: *I found the cutest outfit. This one has bumblebees on it which fits your motif.*

She sent a picture of a bumblebee onesie, and I shook my head before showing it to Luca.

"How many bumblebee outfits will this child have?" Luca asked with a laugh.

"I have no idea. But it makes my mom happy. And at least she's stopped trying to learn to knit."

Luca shook his head and looked over at the half-finished blanket behind me on the armchair. "It could be worse."

"Yes, it could have caught on fire," I said, before texting my mom back that it looked cute, and setting my phone down.

"That was really nice of Ashleigh's parents, you know. Sending that blanket that she made?"

It had come two days prior, and I hadn't brought it up, nor had Luca, but as I looked over at the couch, at the beautifully knitted yellow-and-cream blanket, I reached out and gripped Luca's hands.

For some reason I was nervous, but then again I knew exactly why I should be.

Because Ashleigh's parents had sent a baby blanket. Meaning Ashleigh's parents knew I was pregnant.

I hated that I was jealous of a dead woman.

"Ashleigh's parents are good people. They're grandparents themselves from Ashleigh's two older siblings. And, I don't know, I guess they wanted to do something to show that they're happy for me." He shrugged, before leaning forward to kiss me gently on the lips.

"I know you didn't read the note, but she made sure to say that she started this when she heard about the pregnancy, rather than finishing something that she started for her."

"Am I really that transparent?"

"Of course not. But it is a little weird. I'm really sorry that you never got to meet Ashleigh, because I think you guys would have been friends."

I glared at him. "I don't know about that."

"Honestly, Devney reminds me a little of her sometimes."

My eyebrow shot up. "Really? You never said that."

"Just in some of her mannerisms, but she was her own person, just like you and Devney are your own people. Paisley too, but I always feel weird about bringing her up, considering her and August."

I nodded, completely understanding. August and Paisley were getting along as well as they could, but there was still something there. Or maybe I just wanted something there so it would complete our friendship set nicely. But Paisley was still in a serious relationship with Jacob, and I wasn't going to broach that subject.

"Anyway, Ashleigh's parents just wanted to give us a gift, to make sure that I knew that they were happy for me. It's been years, Addison. I'm really okay, you know. I love being here and I'm really excited to be a dad and try to not screw up this child's life. I mean, I don't really have a great track record when it comes to parents; thank God your parents know what they're doing."

I shook my head and laughed, warmth filling me. "My parents are pretty great. And I'm really glad that your parents haven't stopped by. I know that's mean, but I am really happy about that."

They had not contacted us at all since hearing about the pregnancy. I knew Luca had no idea what they were doing, or even if they were back in town. It didn't matter. Because this kid, whoever they may be, was going to have a huge family no matter what.

"I'm glad that you and Ashleigh's parents seem to be finding your new path."

"I don't know if I'll ever speak to them again. Not that I wouldn't want to, just that they're from a different chapter of my life, one that's closed. And they're very happy with their grandkids and their kids. And Ashleigh's always going to be part of my memories, but I'm looking forward to the future. With the two of you."

I wanted to say something, wanted to tell him that I loved him, and this seemed almost like the perfect time.

This *was* the fucking perfect time.

"Help me stand up?" I asked. Because I didn't want to be sitting when I finally did the one thing I should have done months ago.

Tell him what I felt.

He frowned as he helped me stand, still shirtless and wearing those gray sweatpants that just did everything to me.

"Luca," I said just as an odd snapping sound echoed through my brain.

Warmth spread through me again, but this time it was different. It didn't hurt, it was just weird, and then wetness slid between my legs, and I let out a shocked gasp, staggering back as Luca gripped my arms and looked between us.

"Oh my God," he said quickly.

"Luca. My water."

"Holy hell. Okay. I know what to do. I have the phone tree. Or the group chat. And I need a shirt. Let me get a shirt. You stand right there."

Before I could panic, because he was clearly panicking for the both of us, he let out a deep breath, cupped my face, and kissed me.

Tears pricked my eyes as he leaned back and looked at me.

"The baby's coming. I can't wait." And then he leaned down, kissed my belly, and ran off, presumably to go start our birth plan. I put my hands over my stomach, feeling the back pain that I had been ignoring throughout most of the day.

"Welcome home, baby. Let's do this."

Because I was about to have a baby with my best friend.

The panic over that finally started to hit.

Chapter Sixteen

Luca

"Are you sure you're doing okay? I can go get you some more ice chips."

Addison sat up, her hands on her belly as she breathed slowly in and out. Her hair, which had grown a bit longer over the past few months, was now braided back into two French braids and twisted somehow in the back so it was all away from her face. She looked so damn pretty, even with her red nose and glaring eyes. I knew she was in pain, and was just as scared as I was, but I had a feeling she was handling this far better than me.

Which meant I needed to get my ass into gear and not screw up.

"I don't need any ice chips. If you want to keep pacing, you're welcome to do that. I know that helps sometimes."

"I feel like I heard sarcasm in that tone."

"Oh, there was plenty of sarcasm in that tone. I'm fine. I'm just sitting here, wondering when this baby is going to be pushed out through my vagina. Which apparently is going to hurt more than the lower back pain and contractions already hurt."

I sat down in the chair next to her and took her hand, rubbing her palm with my thumb. "So you had no idea you were in labor?" I asked, still confused.

I had grabbed the bag and everything we had prepped while Addison texted the group chats. Paisley and Devney were going to handle everything on that end after that, according to our birth plan, so all I had to do was make sure I had everything in the car, including Addison.

The fact that I'd almost forgotten Addison at the house notwithstanding. She stood at the front door as I had packed everything in the car, just giving me a look.

I blushed, double checked we had our phone chargers, and then we were in the car and heading towards the hospital.

Now we were sitting in our room, both of us waiting for this next part of this adventure.

No, this wasn't stressful at all.

"No, I didn't. I just had back pain. I've been uncomfortable this entire pregnancy because I haven't been able to go out and do what I want, like baby yoga or whatever else pregnant women do. I've been at the house watching you prep the nursery. Watching you paint the walls and get everything ready. I sat down in that same armchair I've been stuck in for months, even during my baby shower as my best friends brought everyone to me and I wasn't allowed to lift a finger. And now we're here and it's all coming to an end and yet something huge is beginning and I'm really stressed out."

I leaned forward and cupped her face with my free hand, my other one still holding hers.

"Do you want me to tell you that you've got this? That you are strong and capable and no matter what you can handle it? Because you know that, Addison. You are the most fierce and competent and strong and beautiful woman that I know. I've loved watching you thrive in this, even though this wasn't the plan you had when you thought about having a kid. But you've got this. And I'm going to be right beside you."

"You've been beside me this whole time, you know. It's a little daunting."

I raised a brow. "I'm daunting?"

"Maybe? But it's more the fact that you're here. And I never doubted you would be. Which is probably something I should worry about."

I leaned forward and took her lips, pressing my forehead to hers as we each rested for a moment.

"I think another contraction's coming."

She squeezed down on my hand as she breathed out like we had practiced during our class, the midwife having come to the house to work with her.

I hated that I hadn't been able to get her out of the house more while still making sure she was safe. I was a doctor, but not for people. I wasn't able to do much for her, and I hated that.

She had been on bedrest for two trimesters and hadn't been able to have the pregnancy she deserved. But it was the pregnancy that she had gone through, was going through, so I held her hand through the contraction, and wiped away her tears and sweat, and let her curse me out.

"I hate you, you know," she growled, running her hands over her stomach.

"I hate myself too. This is all my fault."

"It really is. I mean, seriously? Why does your sperm have to be so amazing?"

"I feel like I came into the room at the wrong time," Paisley said, and I burst out laughing.

"You really did."

"So I take it everything's normal?"

"As normal as you can be for the fact that I'm only four inches dilated."

I winced, feeling that somehow this was my fault again.

Paisley studied both of us. "And you somehow blame yourself for the fact that you're not progressing as quickly as you wanted to? You're doing great. I have an entire room of people here that want updates by the way, and since I won the coin toss to be able to come back here, I'm going to switch places with Luca."

Panic settled in my chest. "What?"

"Go take a breather, I'll stay here with soon-to-be Mom."

Addison's eyes widened. "Mom. Wow. That's going to be soon. I'm going to be a mom." She beamed as she looked towards me. "Right, Daddy?"

"Now I'm having another panic attack even though we've already talked about the fact that yes there's a baby coming. I will go see the others."

I cupped her face and kissed her softly, knowing that these would be some of the last moments with just the two of us. Even with Paisley in the room, it was just the two of us. Life was about to change forever, altered into a new reality that didn't make any sense and yet made the best sense.

This was going to be amazing.

Even if it scared the hell out of me.

"I'll be right back."

"And maybe bring those ice chips."

"Anything you need."

Walking away was one of the hardest things I'd ever done, even though I knew I'd be right back. It was just so hard to leave her in pain, when all I wanted to do was ensure that she was safe and happy.

The doctors and nurses were constantly in and out, making sure that she was comfortable and her blood pressure was doing well.

Other than that first complication, she had been fine. She hadn't passed out again, and we had followed the doctor's orders implicitly. I knew she was tired of sitting in that damn room and dealing with my ugly face every day.

But I had moved in to take care of her, and that's exactly what I had done.

The fact that she let me have animals in and out all

the time because of my job, and was just always there for me no matter what? That meant something.

I just wasn't sure what we were going to do once the baby came.

But that point was moot, because I wasn't going anywhere.

She was it for me.

And this baby? It changed everything. For the better, and for the stress, but I couldn't wait. Even as I panicked because I was about to be a dad.

I walked out into the waiting room and smiled as everyone looked up at me.

"Everything okay? Paisley went in there to relieve you for a bit."

"And we have food for you," Devney said as she waddled towards me.

She was heavily pregnant and due in one week. "I love you. But should you be standing?"

"I'm okay. I'm here for my new niece or nephew, and I brought you food to take care of you. And I knew if you ate it anywhere near Addison, she would murder you."

"That is the truth," I said as I took the bag from her.

I opened it up and smiled at the burrito and chips and queso.

"The smells delicious."

"It should be, I picked it out," August said, which made me grin.

"I'm going to scarf this down quickly and head back in there. I want to make sure she's okay."

"Paisley is texting, so don't worry. She's doing just fine," Devney said.

"Are we late?"

I had just taken a big bite of burrito so I could only wave at Addison's parents.

They looked relieved to see me as they came over.

"Oh good, you're getting a break. I was really afraid that you were going to exhaust yourself just like you've been doing these past months taking care of our daughter."

Over the past few months I had really gotten to know the Lilys. They were great people who loved their daughter. And I knew they were relieved that she finally had a job she loved, and maybe relieved that I was with her.

Not that I was going to ask them that.

"I'm just eating something real quick."

"Because our daughter would kick you in the nuts if you decided to eat in front of her when she's not allowed to," Addison's dad said, and August laughed beside me.

"That sounds like Addison."

"Do you think she'd want us to go on back?" Addison's mom asked. "I know in the birthing plan it's just the two of you. Do you know how far she's dilated?"

I swallowed my food before answering. "Four centimeters."

"Oh, damn," Devney said with a wince.

"I really don't know why I have to know these things," August put in. "I mean, there should be things I shouldn't know about the mother of my future niece or nephew."

I scowled at my brother, though he was just trying to lighten the tension in the room.

We were all worried. Worried about the baby, about what was going to happen next. Worried about everything.

But after months of being stressed out about what could happen, the time was here.

"I'm just going to go on back. You stay here," Addison's mother said to her husband. She kissed his cheek and went to go talk to the nurse.

"You're all on the list to go back there," I said.

"We know, we got the spreadsheet," August replied with a roll of his eyes as he handed over some water.

"Stay hydrated. Because if you pass out during the birth, Addison will never let you live it down. Hell, I'd never let you live it down."

"You really are the sweetest."

"I try."

The doors opened again and a family I didn't recognize walked in, so I focused back on my meal.

"I just, I don't know what I'll do if something happens," I whispered, and I hadn't even realized I was saying the words until they were already out.

"Don't think about it. If you think about it, you'll stress yourself out for no reason."

I frowned at Heath.

"I don't know, it seems like a good reason to be stressed."

"Well, just be there for her. Worry about what you can do and not about what you can't."

I finished my food and went to wash my hands. When I came back, everybody was silent, and I realized that other people had joined the party.

Only it didn't feel like a party right then.

My sister came forward and hugged me tightly.

"Sorry we're late. We were dealing with a few of Ford's family things."

I looked up at Ford, who shrugged. "I'll talk about it later. But it's baby time now. Congratulations, brother."

I hugged Ford, then Noah, then both Greer's husbands moved back to let my baby sister hold me tight.

"By the way, I'm so sorry. They followed us. Long story."

I frowned then looked past her and realized why everybody was stressed. My parents stood in the corner, not touching, but also not looking as if they were planning to leave anytime soon.

I opened my mouth to say something, only nothing came out.

"We wanted to be here. But we can go if you want us to," my mom said, and I looked at Heath who appeared just as flabbergasted as I felt, and then at August who glared.

It was Greer who spoke up. "As long as they're polite, I'll handle it." She beamed at me. "That's what sisters are for."

"I have to go back there."

"Go forth and take care of her. We've got you, Dad," she teased, though I saw the worry in her eyes.

For me? For Addison? For the fact that the parents that I hadn't spoken to in months were here together?

I didn't know why they were here. But maybe their need to be involved overrode the fact that they're selfish asses.

"I'll keep everyone updated and send Paisley back out."

"Sounds like a plan," August grumbled, as another

person walked in that I recognized as Paisley's boyfriend.

I didn't know Jacob well, and I nodded at him as he went over to sit next to August, like that wasn't awkward at all.

But I didn't have time for my family drama, not when my new family was about to arrive.

I made way back inside and Addison glared.

"You ate. That's queso on your lip."

I quickly wiped my mouth, and then looked down at my hands. "It was not. I washed my face."

"Well, I can smell it. I can't believe you had a burrito."

"I need the strength to keep up with you. You're the strongest person I know. I'm weak."

"Keep going. I think that's working," Paisley said with a laugh as she made her way to the door.

"I'll keep everyone updated, and I'll rotate them in and out."

"Not everyone," I grumbled, and Paisley nodded.

Well, apparently the group chat was caught up.

Good. Because this was fucking weird.

"What's wrong?" Addison asked as I sat down next to her.

"Nothing."

"You're lying. So tell me."

"My parents are in the waiting room. So are yours by the way."

"I know, my mom just came back. You must have just missed her."

I frowned, having forgotten that.

"Oh. Well."

"As for your parents, good. They can be here for you for a minute, until they make it all about them and then they can leave. It doesn't matter. They're going to be grandparents no matter what. How much they're in our child's life? That's on us. Not them. It's an amazing thing. I'm so fucking protective right now that I know that we're going to protect this kid no matter what."

"Damn straight." I leaned forward and kissed her.

I wanted to tell her that I loved her, that this was it, but I knew she would probably think that this was just because of the hormones and the situation.

So I would wait.

Even though I really wanted to tell her.

It took hours. Hours of sweat, ice chips, and pain.

The family circled in and out, each taking their turns to tell Addison how good she was doing, and then she was ten centimeters and fully effaced, things I knew way too much about now, and suddenly everything happened quickly.

They got her into position, and then I was holding

her hand as the love of my life screamed and pushed, and a wriggling little whatever-covered baby started screeching, screaming its little lungs out, and I let the tears finally fall.

Keeley Lily Cassidy was born at 3:01 a.m. on a Tuesday.

After everyone was cleaned up, and our baby passed all her first tests, I found myself sitting in the large hospital bed next to Addison, her leaning against me and Keeley snuggled up to Addison's breasts.

"She's so beautiful. So tiny."

I kissed the top of Addison's head, then reached out to slide my finger along Keeley's cheek. She was so small, her hand barely big enough to wrap around my thumb.

"How's this even possible? She wasn't here a couple hours ago, now she's here, and I would break the world for her."

"Same. Everything's changed, Luca. We're parents."

"Damn straight."

"We should probably stop cursing."

"I think we can keep cursing for a little bit. She probably heard enough of it when she was in the womb."

"This means I'm not on bed rest anymore, and we

can finally show this baby girl the world. That we can do everything."

"Are we going to tell her that she started off because of a birthday?"

"Maybe not the drunken part."

"What about the fake part?" I asked, smiling as she beamed over at me.

She was so damn beautiful.

"Maybe she'll like the fake part. I mean, telling her that her daddy was also her mommy's fake fiancé? That's a good story."

I leaned forward and took her lips with mine.

"I love you, Addison."

She swallowed and looked up at me, the words having taken far too long to come out.

The words that meant everything.

"I should have told you long ago. That you're everything to me. But I was so afraid that if I did, you would only think it was because of Keeley, or because we needed each other. But I want you to know that I love you and I cannot wait to raise this baby girl with you. I told you I would do anything for you, and I mean it. But the first thing I'm going to do is fight for you. There's nothing fake about what I feel for you. There hasn't been for a long time. I love you, Addison. I loved you before Keeley, and I'll love you with her."

Addison sniffed and I wiped the tears from her cheeks.

She didn't say anything for so long, a sense of foreboding slid over me.

Was I wrong? Did she not love me back? Had I said the wrong thing?

I wasn't sure what I was supposed to say. How to fix this. But me hiding from what we were and what we could be didn't make sense anymore. It hadn't for a long time.

"I love you too. I never took off the ring, you know. Even when my fingers started to swell and then they stopped doing that whole swelling thing. Thankfully. I'm still wearing it."

I looked down at her hand and realized she had put the ring back on, since she had taken off all her jewelry for the birth.

I looked back up at her. "It's a damn good ring."

"Language," she whispered.

"I'll do better. Promise."

"So, let's see, we accidentally slept together the first time, had a fake relationship the second time, you accidentally moved in the third time, and now here we are, holding a very real baby."

"And my feelings are very real. I know neither of us are good about saying that. I've been so afraid of doing that, but I'm going to do better from now on. I promise. I love you both. And the entire family's about to rush in here, and it's going to be loud and we're going to have to figure out how to be parents together, but we'll do that."

Loud and messy and real.

"I think I hear them running down the halls, so I guess these last-minute I love yous are a good thing."

I laughed, kissing her softly.

"I was your last-minute boyfriend, your last-minute fiancé, and your last-minute roommate."

"I don't mind."

The room filled and we showed off our daughter to our family, and I knew that I should have said that long ago. That holding back had been a mistake.

So I would prove to her that she was mine. That I deserved to be in her life.

I would never let Addison feel that she wasn't good enough, that she was second choice. That she was last minute.

And Keeley would always know that she was first. That she was loved.

Because somehow, without trying, I had found my new family. My reason to be here.

And that was something I would never take for granted, even by accident.

Chapter Seventeen

Addison

Two months later

I tiptoed across the living room floor, doing my best to not make a sound. Although I could hear soft breathing over the baby monitor, Keeley did not sleep hard enough for me to be stomping around the living room and making noise.

And while I did my best to do things like vacuum or

dishes while she slept so she would get used to it, she had been cranky and sniffly all day, so I wanted to make sure that she got her beauty rest.

Of course, that meant I stepped on a stuffed animal that had a squeaker inside, and as I gently released my foot and the squeak echoed in the living room, I cringed.

But there were no additional sounds from the nursery, just soft baby sleeping noises.

I sighed in relief and continued on my way back to the bedroom.

It had been two months since our lives had changed. Two months since everything had changed once again.

Luca had never moved back home. He just stayed, and I was never going to let that man leave.

I hadn't meant to fall in love with him, hadn't meant for him to be by my side and to be with me, but there was no going back from that.

Because, he had wanted to stay.

The short-term rental of his place was now over, and we were slowly moving some of his furniture over, which in some cases was better than mine. Blending two households wasn't easy, and it was something I'd never done before. But I was really enjoying the process.

He had his armchair over in the corner near mine, although I was pretty sure I wanted to burn mine, as I had spent most of my pregnancy in that damn thing. But it was still nice and comfortable to rock in while watching TV with Keeley on my chest.

I didn't know what we were going to do with all of his furniture, since this house wasn't big enough for the additional office that we would eventually need. We had enough space for now, as long as we used the storage unit for some furniture.

We were going to put his house on the market soon, but we didn't really have time to deal with that right then.

Paisley had already offered to take care of it for us, because her and Devney could seriously just take over the world together, and I was so excited to get back to work and help do that.

My maternity leave was almost over, and soon I would be taking baby Keeley into work with me. Devney was still on maternity leave as well, and baby Hayleigh was the most adorable cousin that Keeley could ever ask for.

Soon Paisley's company would have two additional babies under its roof during the day.

Heath didn't work each weekday, and I knew he was changing his hours so he could have weekends off completely to match with Devney's. They had hired more team members so Heath and his family could really enjoy their time. Plus, they were expanding by opening an additional business, this one more focused on food, and I knew Paisley had a hand in that because that woman could seriously do anything.

I wasn't sure how Heath and Devney were doing it, but they were.

Just as Luca and I were.

While I wasn't working, because I was actually taking time off, I could work from home if I needed to, but I really was excited to go back to the office. I liked being around people.

And while we had occasional animals in our house because of Luca's job, we did get our own puppy named Puddles, who was currently out on a walk with the man that I loved.

Puddles was a mixed breed, though Luca did say that some chocolate lab was involved.

He was an adorable little mess and I loved him. Even though he came by his name honestly. Hence the long walk.

Why we decided to take home an abandoned puppy and the baby all at the same time I would never know, but who needed sleep anyway?

Luca and his partner had added a new vet to their business, and they had the space for the additional office, so they didn't have to build on like Heath was doing.

It was a little crazy, and I couldn't believe that we were all doing so much.

But it was all about working towards our future, something I was truly excited about, truly blessed to have.

I honestly never thought that this was what my life would be. That I would not only be a mother, that I would be living with the man that I loved.

We weren't engaged and hadn't actually discussed marriage. It wasn't that either of us were scared of it, at least I didn't think so, but we had more important things on our plate than a wedding ceremony.

Just knowing that I loved him and he loved me and that we were raising our daughter together was enough for me for now.

Maybe one day I would get on one knee and surprise a proposal on him. That might be fun.

I stepped into the nursery where Keeley slept and smiled over at our daughter.

She was so cute, Cupid-bow lips and long eyelashes. She looked just like Luca, but he kept saying she looked like me.

All I knew was that she was my everything. Our touchstone. And I would do all in my power to protect her and be worthy of her.

I left her to sleep, aware that the moment she woke

up she would probably be hungry and our evening plans would shift.

I made my way back into the bedroom and started to get ready for Luca's return. He was currently on a walk with Puddles, but when he came back, it would be time.

It had to be.

It had been months since we had touched.

And it wasn't because I didn't want to. Okay, sex had been the furthest thing on my mind recently, but still, I could count on one hand the number of times that Luca and I had slept together, because of circumstances outside of our control. But the doctor gave me the all clear, and I was going to lean into that with every ounce of anticipation I could possibly have.

So I slathered myself with lotion, a dab of perfume here and a dab of perfume there. I put on a silky little number that I had never worn before—a gift from Paisley and Devney and I was grateful that they had gone one size up because my breasts were freaking huge.

They had gotten big during pregnancy, but now that I was breastfeeding? Ridiculously huge. As soon as Luca untied that little bow, I'd pop out, breasts going everywhere.

Though I was pretty sure he'd like that.

The dress went down to mid-thigh, and I had little boy short panties on that were just made of lace. I wasn't really into thongs, but I figured he'd have fun unwrapping me.

I slid on the robe that came with it, which wasn't see through, and was almost a little modest until you realized how short it was.

I was ready for Luca, so I just needed the man to get home.

And as if I had thought him into existence, the back door opened and I heard Luca whispering to Puddles.

"Okay, we have to be quiet. Be quiet."

"Yip yip yip."

I smiled, then groaned as Keeley made a whimpering sound.

I quickly ran to the door, but then realized she was back to sleeping, as Puddles had quit his tiny little barks.

"Okay, we're going to go into your play area for a minute, hopefully maybe more than a minute. However, it has been a long while."

I put my hand over my mouth so I wouldn't laugh out loud as Luca set up Puddles with playtime and water, and I knew I probably wouldn't last a minute either.

For two people who had accidentally fallen into each other multiple times, the fact that we had scheduled this moment? Oh, how our lives had changed.

Luca turned the corner down the hallway and

nearly tripped over his feet, his mouth hanging open in shock.

That's when I remembered exactly what I was wearing, and blushed.

I tugged at the bottom of the robe, my teeth biting into my lip. "I was going to surprise you," I said quietly.

Luca's eyes went dark, and his throat worked as he swallowed.

"Consider me surprised."

And before I could blink, he was on me, his mouth on mine, his taste exquisite.

We had kissed of course, had been very careful these months to keep it just kissing.

He hadn't let me touch him over this time, even though I had offered to watch him jerk off.

Now though, it was all I could do not to crawl over him like a monkey and let him devour me.

He grabbed my hips and lifted me with such ease that I let out a shocked breath.

And then my legs were wrapped around his waist and he was carrying me to the bedroom.

"Tell me when it's too much. Just tell me if you need to stop."

I shook my head, my feet going to the floor as he set me down.

"Just remember, this is post baby. My body's

different."

"Darling, love of my life, I have seen every inch of you over the past few months. I know exactly what your body looks like, and I love every ounce of you. I don't care that you don't look exactly like you did a year ago. Hell, I don't look like I did a year ago."

I raised a brow. "Your arms have more muscles; you look even more built than before and I kind of hate that about you."

He rolled his eyes. "Because I've been jerking off enough that I now have forearm muscles. I have to alternate hands so I don't end up with one Popeye arm and one skinny arm."

I put my hand over my mouth again, trying not to laugh and wake up the baby, but then he was undoing the belt on my robe and the fabric fell to the ground.

His eyes looked like they were ready to boggle out of his head, and he licked his lips.

"It's not even Christmas yet."

"Well, you should unwrap your present anyway."

He grinned, and then undid the bow between my breasts. My breasts popped out, full and heavy, my nipples hard points.

He groaned as he cupped me in his hands.

"Your tits have always been beautiful, but right now? I think I'm in love."

"Oh, we're going to have so much fun."

He leaned down and pressed a gentle kiss on each breast, before setting me back on the bed, legs spread, as he kissed and sucked down my body and nearly sent me over the edge.

When he finished unwrapping me, leaving me naked, I groaned, tugging on his shirt.

"As hot as it is with you dressed and me naked, I need to see you."

"As you wish," he whispered, and then his shirt was off and his hand was between my legs.

I was already swollen, aching for him, and when his fingers found my clit, gently rubbing circles over me, I arched off the bed, coming so quickly I surprised myself.

My toes curled, and he grinned down at me.

"You're so stunning. Your whole body flushed with that; I love seeing you come."

"It has been way too long."

"Then I won't make you wait any longer for the next one."

He shucked off his pants and was between my legs, gently teasing me and kissing me nearly to the edge again.

He was hard and ready and when he positioned himself at my entrance, both of us sucked in a breath.

"Ready?" he asked, and I nodded, no words available to me.

Because he was so big, and it had been a long time, and I didn't care.

As he slid deep inside of me, I realized everything was different. Not because of my body or the way life changed, but because *we* were different.

This was the man that I loved. The man that I wanted to be with until the end of days.

And this wasn't just a hard fuck over a fun night. This was what I had been craving. What I'd been missing even though I hadn't realized I'd been missing it at all.

At least not until it was almost too late.

I wrapped my legs around him as he pumped in and out of me, slowly at first and then harder. I raked my nails down his back as he plunged into me.

And when I came again, he followed me, quick and fast and both of us sweating and panting.

He rolled to the side, still deep inside of me, as we just looked at each other.

"I was not expecting to go *that* quick," he said with a laugh.

I kissed his shoulder, holding him close.

"We'll just have to keep practicing. I'm a little rusty."

"Oh no, you're fucking great. So great that I came

way too quickly."

"No no. I just had two orgasms. We're not trying to set records here."

"We've got a lifetime to keep setting them."

My eyes filled with happy tears as I smiled at him.

"That sounds like a plan."

We cleaned each other up, laughing as we dressed. And then Luca went to go let out Puddles so the puppy could play around the house, and I smiled and made my way back into the nursery.

I frowned when Keeley started to cry because it sounded different from her other cries, her hands outstretched for me.

I moved over to her, putting my hand on her forehead, and my heart froze.

"Luca, I think she has a fever."

Luca was there in an instant as I picked up Keeley, letting the baby scream against me. She was such an easy baby, so happy all the time. She slept at night and was just so sweet.

These cries tore at me and made me want to cry right along with her.

"I got the thermometer. Let's see."

I walked around the room, trying to figure out what to do. I held her in my arms, but she wouldn't stop crying. She was sweaty and looked so sad.

"101."

"She was fine less than an hour ago. She was stuffy, but didn't have a fever. We checked. She was fine. And then we're over here just taking time for ourselves and our baby is crying."

"She didn't start crying until just now. Come on, let's call the pediatrician and we'll go in to see them okay?"

My heart stopped as I looked at him.

"We need to go into the hospital?"

"The baby has a fever, so we're going to go in and get some medicine. I'm sure it's just a bug."

"But you don't know that."

"Everything is fine. I love you. I'm going to take care of you both. Let me just call my brother so he can take care of Puddles in case we are gone for a while, and then we're going to grab our things and take Keeley to the doctor, okay?"

"Okay. You're not panicking. So she's okay, right?" I asked with my heart racing.

"I'm not panicking because we've got this. And me panicking is not going to help you. So grab her bag and get her ready to go, and I'm going to get us there okay? We've got this. I love you, Addison. We've got this."

He kissed my forehead, and I reached out to grab his hand.

"Thank you for being steady."

"Always. I get to panic next time though, okay? Like if I stub my toe? We can take turns."

My lips twitched, but I nodded.

Because all along this path, even when I'd had to lie to my former boss about my relationship, or when we had first found out we were pregnant. I had been scrambling for control. But Luca had always been steady. He had gone through hell before, and found his way out of it, and I was learning that he was going to be panicking deep inside, so I would be there for him when it finally burst out.

Because yes indeed, we would be taking turns. Struggling as we figured out the next step.

It only took a few minutes, and the pediatrician did want us to head to the hospital with that kind of fever, so I sat in the passenger seat, looking in the mirror we set up so I could see our baby's rear-facing car seat.

Her red face was all scrunched up as she cried, and my heart broke.

"I should have sat in the back with her. Why am I up here?"

"I can pull over if you want to go back there, but we're only ten minutes away, okay?"

"Okay. This is fine. You're okay baby," I whispered,

knowing that she could see my eyes between the two mirrors.

I had no idea how my parents or their parents had ever dealt with babies in cars and in life without so many mirrors and apps.

I just wanted my baby to be okay, and I didn't like not knowing what was wrong. It was just a cold, probably, but what if it was something worse?

"I texted Devney, and she's making sure that Hayleigh's okay. They had a play date a couple of days ago."

A play date with two-month-olds didn't actually mean a play date, but we wanted them to be best friends and would see each other often.

But now I was so afraid that I'd gotten their baby sick.

"And?" Luca asked as he took a turn.

"And Hayleigh seems to be fine, but they're going to keep an eye out. And they want updates. The group chat's going insane."

Between Greer, Ford, Noah, my parents, Paisley, Heath, Devney, and August, there were more than enough people in the chat. The fact that we had separate chats for nearly everybody in random groups just meant that my phone was blowing up, but I ignored it for now.

I didn't have any updates for them.

"Okay, we're almost there."

Luca stopped at a stop sign, and when it was time to go he moved forward, when suddenly a horn blasted out of nowhere.

I turned to the left as Luca cursed, slamming the brakes, but it was too late.

The sound of metal screeching echoed in my ear, and I shouted for Luca, for Keeley.

All I knew was that someone had just hit us, running a stop sign, and my baby was crying.

"Is everyone okay?" Luca asked, as he turned around, his eyes wide.

We hadn't even been going fast enough for the airbags to deploy, but I scrambled out of the car, Luca following me.

"I'm so sorry, I'm so sorry," the teenage boy shouted as he started to get out of his car, but I ignored him, running around the car and opening up the door to get to Keeley.

"Baby it's okay, baby it's okay."

She was still crying even though she didn't look to be hurt, but for all I knew she had been jostled and now she was hurting even more and I didn't know what to do.

I reached out and cupped her face, trying not to let my own tears fall.

"Mom is here. Mom is here."

"I am a nurse. Is there anything I can do?" one of the passersby said as they got out of their car, and I turned to her.

"We were on the way to the hospital because my two-month-old baby has a fever and won't stop crying, and now this."

I pointed at the teenage boy, anger in my tone.

He flinched, but I didn't care.

I would feel bad for him later, because it looked to be just an accident, but my baby could be hurt.

"You're going to want to stand back," Luca growled at the kid. "I'm sure you didn't mean it, but I'm not in the fucking mood right now."

I'd never loved that man more.

"Okay, let's see what I can do."

"I already called 911, just in case," another woman said, phone to her ear. "How old is the baby?"

"Two months," I repeated.

Everything moved quickly after that, as people from all over the neighborhood seemed to come over to make sure we were okay.

It was a small fender bender, neither car damaged too much.

The nurse was checking out Keeley, and then the ambulance arrived and took over for her.

I slid my hand into Luca's and he pulled me close to his side.

"We're okay. We're okay."

I pressed my lips together and nodded, knowing that we had to be.

It was just a little car accident, something that happened every day.

Usually, it wouldn't even matter, but my family was in that car.

I could have lost everyone today, and I could barely catch my breath.

By the time we got to the hospital I was panicking again, hating myself for it. I could handle almost any high-powered situation at work, and most things in my personal life. But hearing my baby cry? Seeing the fear and anger in Luca's gaze?

I couldn't handle it.

"Are you okay?" Luca asked softly as he looked at me in the hospital room, waiting for the doctor to tell us anything. We didn't have any news about what illness our child had, but we did have an update about the accident. Since we hadn't been going fast, everybody was just fine. But that still didn't make it any easier, it was almost too much to deal with.

"I'm okay. Not even sore in the least."

"I'm just so pissed off at myself for not seeing that

car."

I frowned at him. "It wasn't your fault. You are not the one who hit us. You stopped and looked both ways and that kid hit you."

"I'm just happy we were both going slow enough that it wasn't as bad as it could have been. I would never forgive myself if you guys were hurt because of me. I don't know what I'd do if I lost you or Keeley."

I cursed under my breath because I had been so selfish in my panic over losing him and Keeley that I hadn't thought about what he might be feeling.

I softly touched his face and kissed his chin. "You did everything right. I promise. We're okay."

"I thought I was supposed to be reassuring you."

"How about we reassure each other."

"We can do that. I love you, you know. I am so fucking happy we have each other. I'm not normally an emotional guy, even though sometimes I feel like it with you."

"Oh?" I said with a laugh.

"Yes. Oh. I just get so happy sometimes, so happy that we have what we have, even though we didn't quite ask for it. And I just don't want to lose that."

I pressed my lips together, nodding. "Same here."

"You're never getting rid of me, Addison. You're stuck with me."

"I don't mind. Not at all."

I kissed his chin again, while Keeley slept on the little nursery bed beside us.

When the doctor came in to give us an update, I sagged in relief.

"She doesn't seem shaken up or hurt at all from the accident, and we're going to give her some medicine for her cold to try to get the fever down. We want to keep her overnight, just in case. But that's being overly precautious, and you guys are already here, so let's make sure that we're all on the same page, and she'll be right as rain soon. You have a lovely family," he added at the end, and I wrapped my arm around my best friend's waist and smiled.

We did have a lovely family.

It wasn't what we thought we'd have, it wasn't what we'd planned, but it was exactly what we needed.

I had fallen in love with my best friend, and I had somehow manifested him into being my boyfriend, my fiancé, and the father of my child. And not in that order. I knew that, no matter what, I would forever be grateful, I would forever know that this was what I had chosen, subconsciously or not.

This was my family. My future, my everything.

And I couldn't wait to make more memories with my best friend.

Chapter Eighteen

Luca

"There's nothing like cold fried chicken on an afternoon picnic. Don't you think?"

I looked over at Heath and raised a brow. "Did you utter that sentence unironically? That doesn't sound like you."

Heath shrugged. "What? We're new dads. We're supposed to enjoy this shit."

I looked down at the babies in the covered bassinet between us that were sleeping after a lovely afternoon of giggling and screaming their little heads off. Although at three months I didn't know if it was giggling and smiling or if it was just them filling their diapers. Honestly it could be either.

I had never imagined myself as a father like this. I had never imagined that when we moved from Portland to Denver, this would be my life. We had come here to be with Greer and to start over. Each of us had started over in our way. Greer with her business and her husbands. Heath with his business as well, having wanted to see if he could make it with his friend rather than at the place he had sold out west. And he wanted to start over with all of us as the big brother he was.

I had needed a change when I could start my career as a vet, and I needed to get away from a place that had so many memories. I still thought of Ashleigh from time to time, as she had been my friend and a girl that I loved. But I wasn't in love with her anymore. That distinction had taken a long time for me to figure out. But it was something that made my love for Addison all the more clear.

You were allowed to have more than one love in your life.

Just because you didn't have the life you thought you would didn't mean your life wasn't worth living. And that had taken me a long time to figure out.

Or at least longer than I had planned.

Now I was a father, in love with a woman I never thought I would have, and damn happy about it.

Yes, I was still working far too many hours, but we knew that would happen as we added more people to the company. It helped that we had a support system here with our family, hence why we had moved here to begin with.

August had started over as well with his career, but running from his problems didn't seem to be working out the way he wanted.

Especially since Paisley was now part of our daily lives.

Considering that both Addison and Devney worked with Paisley, and their partnership was only growing leaps and bounds as time went on, we knew that she would be part of our lives for a long damn time. And somehow August was going to have to deal with it.

I sipped my beer as I looked over at our other brother and shook my head.

"Still okay?" Heath asked. "I mean, I know that this isn't what we expected, but I love what we're doing out here. I love my family. I love my wife, I'm just happy. And yes, that includes eating cold fried chicken."

"You're right, cold fried chicken is good. Especially with this beer. And with sleeping babies between us." I froze and looked down at said sleeping babies, and then over at Heath who scowled at me.

We knew the unwritten rule was that we never woke a sleeping baby, or mentioned a sleeping baby, or they would wake and there'd be screaming and whatever else, like diapers. So many diapers. I didn't realize babies could have so many diapers, but this whole father thing was a learning curve, and I was figuring it out.

"Who did August bring this time? Jessica? Francesca? Frankie?" Heath scowled and I rolled my eyes.

"This one is Rebecca."

"Just another of the endless line of women that August seems to be bringing around the family. That seems smart. Really healthy."

I shook my head. "I don't know how he does it. But then again, Addison's only my second girlfriend. I'm really not good at the whole sowing your oats thing he seems to be doing."

"I did enough of that in Portland, and maybe when I first moved here, but then I met Devney and there was no turning back."

"Even for the year you didn't even know you were together," I teased. My brother flipped me off and I laughed.

"You think this one will stick?" I asked, knowing the answer.

"Considering that he's glaring at Paisley and Jacob right now? Probably not."

"You think Jacob's going to stick with Paisley?" I asked. Then I paused. "Why am I asking these things? Since when am I into relationship gossip?"

"Since you became a happy father and happy boyfriend. And to answer your question, I don't know but the two of them seem nice together. I don't know if Jacob fits in with us, though. He's a little too political. You know, that old money type."

I nodded. "He doesn't seem to have a problem with Greer's two husbands."

"Good, because if he did we'd have to beat his ass and I'm not in the mood to go to jail."

"Exactly. Though I'm pretty sure Noah and Ford could kick his ass for us."

"Either way, Paisley looks happy, August looks annoyed, when he is not hiding his emotions, but our girls out there? They look like they're having a fucking great time."

I grinned and followed Heath's gaze to where both Devney and Addison were running barefoot across the soccer field, playing with the middle schoolers.

"I hadn't realized how hot playing soccer in a

sundress could be," I said under my breath, and Heath laughed.

"Don't even get me started," he mumbled.

When Devney passed the ball over to Addison, and Addison kicked a perfect goal right past the twelve-year-old goalkeeper, I threw up my fist and shouted, waking both babies. Of course, Heath had too, so it wasn't completely my fault.

Both women heard their babies' cries, and we waved them off before I picked up Keeley, and Heath picked up Hayleigh.

"You're okay, you're okay. Mommy is just kicking ass and I am a jerk for being loud."

"Stop cursing," Heath grumbled as he rocked Hayleigh back and forth.

We both stood up, walking the babies around as the women came back to the picnic area.

"Is everything okay?" Addison asked, holding out her arms.

"I've got it, just come hold me." I winked and she wrapped her arms around my waist as I used my free arm to put my arm around her shoulder.

I looked up to see Greer taking a photo of us with her phone, and I rolled my eyes.

"How many photos do you have of us today?"

"I'm sorry, but my brother holding a baby and his

girlfriend? It's going to be a photo that I can frame."

She leaned into Noah as Ford leaned down to get them drinks. I smiled, watching our family.

Paisley came over as well and started serving more food, because that woman could never stop moving, as her boyfriend stood off to the side on his phone, a scowl on his face. Then he laughed at something on the other end and looked over at Paisley. She glanced at him and smiled, her shoulders relaxing as he winked at her, his smile bright. He worked long hours with his job, but I knew he spent every free hour with Paisley. They seemed a good fit and, while I knew it would be awkward with August around, Jacob was trying and that had to count for something.

August and Rebecca were over by the parking lot whispering to each other. Rebecca looked happy, and August looked lost in thought again. But then he leaned forward and pushed her hair from her face, a small smile on his face.

Maybe this one would stick longer than a week.

I'd gotten lucky with Addison and we all knew it. Against all odds, I was damn happy. And as everyone talked and ate and I handed off the baby to my sister, I held Addison close and wondered how this was my life.

Soon I would propose, because it was time. And it would be a real one, and she would be my real fiancée.

But she still wore my ring, the fake one that had more memories between us than I ever thought possible. Soon she would be my wife, and I'd make an honest man and woman out of us both. And we would watch our child grow up, and maybe add a sibling or two along the way. We'd stay here. We'd find roots.

I never thought I'd have roots. After all this time, for some reason I thought Denver would be a pit stop. Between grieving and healing, I hadn't expected Addison. I hadn't expected our family.

"What's wrong?" she asked softly, as Greer walked Keeley around the park.

"Just thinking how unexpected life can be. It's pretty good sometimes, you know?"

"I do know. I love you."

"I love you too. Are you ready for work tomorrow?"

She nodded. "We have a huge meeting, and we're going to take over a new company. I'm excited to take over the world."

"That's my girl."

"And you're going to go save some kittens and puppies and maybe a ferret. I'm pretty sure we have the best jobs."

I rolled my eyes. "Maybe not a ferret." Then I paused. "Okay, now that I said that out loud there's probably going to be a ferret. I should probably warn Colt."

She laughed like I wanted her to, and then Keeley was back in my arms, and we were talking about sports and upcoming appointments and dinners and just life.

Life which was unexpected, reality that made so much more sense than dreams.

We weren't perfect, we still fought, and we still made mistakes.

But in the end, we were real.

And I had to smile at the fact that it had started out fake, had started with a broken promise.

But here we were.

I couldn't wait to take the next step and make my fiancée turned girlfriend turned mother of my child into my fiancée again.

I just hoped she'd say yes. Though I had a feeling no was never going to be an answer.

Chapter Nineteen

August

The noise from the dining room increased, so I decided to make my exit. It wasn't that I didn't love my family. I did. I loved them and everything they did. I loved being with them, and had moved here to be with them. I could have stayed in Oregon. It probably would've been easier. I wouldn't have had to deal with getting a new teaching certificate and finding a job that worked for me. I changed schools, had to deal with a whole new set of curriculum, and a whole slew of other issues. But it wasn't as if I thought it would be anything different. It wasn't like I regretted it.

I wasn't sure how I could regret it when I got to be with all of my siblings and their growing families.

We had moved here to be with Greer because our parents had fucked us up enough that we didn't even know our baby sister. But she wasn't a baby any longer. She was married and happy. And my twin, Heath, was a dad, and so was Luca. Their kids were going to grow up running around as best friends, cousins who would never be separated. And yet, somehow the guy who had gotten married first, who thought he had it all set, was left behind.

I rubbed my hand over my face, annoyed with myself. I needed to get out of my head.

I was in a funk and I didn't know why. I shouldn't be jealous that my family was moving on and growing up. I moved here to watch them do that specifically. To be able to participate in their lives, and get over the fact that our parents hated each other. Hated each other enough that they had married not once, not twice, but three times. And were getting divorced. Again.

I didn't know what tether held them together so tight that all they could do was hurt one another. They didn't care that their children were collateral damage.

But honestly, the only good thing that was coming out of this final divorce was that we were going to protect the next generation. Heath's and Luca's kids were not going to have to deal with my parents. I would be the one to stand in front of them all. Greer had already walked away, as our parents couldn't understand the fact that our baby sister had two husbands that loved her and each other. Their relationship wasn't conventional in their eyes—the people who had gotten divorced two, going on three, times were the ones that apparently had a normal relationship and Greer didn't because she happened to be in a throuple. And now we knew that if our parents had a chance, they were going to latch their poisonous and dangerous claws into the next generation and dig in and slowly take away their confidence, their joy, and their sense of what was right and wrong. They would lose the concept of what it meant to be family.

My brothers and sister were just now figuring out what it meant to be family. I thought I'd figured that out once but had been wrong. But that didn't mean I was going to stand by and let my parents hurt them. So I wouldn't.

I would be the first line of defense.

I sighed, listening to everybody enjoy the dinner and party, and went out to the balcony, needing fresh air. The mountain air that came from the Rockies was so crisp, even though we were in a suburb of Denver. If you looked west, all you saw was darkness, and a few tiny lights of cabins in the woods. It was so damn cool. Yes, I loved the trees and the mountains of Portland, being able to see Mount Hood and everything like that, but I loved the Rockies more.

It took a few moments to realize I wasn't alone.

That *she* was there.

It shouldn't be a kick in the gut anymore. Not after so many years. It wasn't like I was the same person that I had been when my ex-wife and I had separated. Paisley was an all-new woman. Strong and gorgeous as ever, with a new shell over that fragility that I had not been able to see in time.

She was close friends with Addison and Devney, so it wasn't as if I could stay away from her. Only I still couldn't quite believe she was here. In Denver, making millions for others and herself. She had become the powerhouse she had always wanted to be.

All she needed to do was watch me walk away to make it happen.

See? Some good things happened when it came to being with me and watching me leave.

She stood there under the moonlight, her shawl tight around her shoulders as she looked up into the sky. Her bright red hair shone under the moonlight, and she looked so damn gorgeous.

Paisley had always taken my breath away with her

high cheekbones, porcelain skin, and curves that filled out a suit and skirt like nobody's business.

She realized she wasn't alone anymore and turned to me, and I didn't let myself think those thoughts anymore.

"How's Jacob?" I asked. I hadn't realized I was going to think it, let alone say the words. They were ridiculous. They shouldn't matter. But they were out there.

Apparently the other man had dug his claws into my psyche and now I couldn't get him out.

She looked at me but didn't frown. That little V between her eyebrows not even making an appearance. She didn't react.

I used to be able to read her face, or perhaps I had lied to myself about thinking I could read her face. Because I hadn't been able to.

I had just been standing in her way.

"He asked me to marry him."

I swallowed hard and tried not to react.

She was going to marry Jacob. That had to be what was coming next. The man who wore business suits and had investors. The man who would probably one day be the governor of Colorado. The man who was just damn good at everything.

The two of them always looked good together,

though I wondered where he was tonight. Why he wasn't at our family dinner when she was.

I broke up with Paisley because we had been too young, and knew even then she was destined for great things, not to be stuck in a rut with a high school teacher with student debt.

We had fought all the fucking time. No matter what we tried, we had fought. But I had never stopped loving her.

Well, hell.

"And?"

She smiled, but it didn't reach her eyes. Why couldn't I read her face anymore? "And I said yes. He loves me. He respects me." When I didn't say anything, she smiled again, but this time I read sadness. Sadness I had put on her face. Because that's what I was good at. "I told myself I wouldn't make the same mistakes I did with my first husband."

The words sounded bitter, so I smirked, doing what I did best. "Glad you are getting your second chance. He's an asshole though. But I guess you're good at choosing assholes."

"I chose you after all." She rolled her eyes, before her shoulders dropped and she sighed. "I don't hate you, August. I stopped doing that a long time ago."

I snorted. Too bad I hated myself.

"Fine. But just leave Pretty Boy Jacob at home when I'm around? I'm not in the mood to deal with his smirking. And I guess you hanging out with your ex-husband and his family probably isn't the best for his political aspects?"

She stared at me and shook her head. "Jealous?" she asked, that biting tone back. I loved that biting tone. It meant there was still some emotion there. Some of the Paisley I remembered.

And yes, I was jealous. But I wasn't going to say it out loud.

"Never."

She searched my face, just like I was searching hers. But I knew she couldn't read me. We were both so good at hiding. That's why it never worked out. Why he was better for her.

"Goodbye, August."

I lifted my chin and met her gaze. "Goodbye, Paisley."

I watched her go, thinking it a bit ironic, as I was the one who had left last time.

I regretted it ever since.

And now it was far too late to fix it. Far too late for second chances.

IF YOU'D LIKE TO READ A BONUS SCENE:
CHECK OUT THIS SPECIAL EPILOGUE!

NEXT IN THE FIRST TIME SERIES:
Things are going to get messy in Second
Chance Husband with Paisley and August.
I can't wait.

Bonus Epilogue

Luca

"I'm just saying, I don't know why you can't play 'I'll Be' by Edward McCain. That is the pinnacle of wedding songs."

I looked at August and blinked, wondering why he was harping on this when we weren't even near the wedding reception yet. I should not have told my brother the name of the song we'd planned on for our first dance.

"'Thinking Out Loud' by Ed Sheeran? Come on, who likes Ed Sheeran?"

I pinched the bridge of my nose and stared at August.

"Are you serious? My future wife, the mother of my child likes Ed Sheeran."

"He was the worst part of *Game of Thrones*."

"And they mentioned him again in the end as the burned redheaded ginger dude because they knew everyone hated him. But he's not singing a random *Game of Thrones* song. It's 'Thinking Out Loud,' which is something that all of us do. It's not our song, because our song is a random rap song from the nineties that doesn't make sense for a first dance."

Heath sighed. "But you're going to play it, aren't you?

"We will be dropping it low. And maybe throwing our hands in the air like we just do not care."

August sighed. "I can't even with you."

"What about 'Iris' by the Goo Goo Dolls?

"While inarguably one of the best songs ever, especially for an emotional and emotive rock ballad, do you not remember that it's from *City of Angels*? And how that ended? I mean, wonderful song, but come on, we want a better happy ever after than that."

"Fine, I will concede that one. But remember that viral video of the guy who said that his dad was on his third or fourth wedding and that was the wedding song he played every single time?"

"Oh, the 'I'll Be' song, the one that you picked? You just threw yourself underneath the bus."

Heath opened his mouth and then closed it, shaking his head. "I do believe that Hayleigh's long nights and colic means I have no idea what the fuck I'm doing. I completely forgot that I was the one that brought him up."

"Is the colic still pretty bad?" I asked.

"She's fine. Honestly, I don't even think it was colic last night, but probably the introduction to solid foods. She's going to be just like her mother, and either completely picky, or want to eat everything. I love it so much." Heath had on that sappy smile of his that I knew matched mine.

I couldn't help but laugh at that. I would forever be grateful that my brother's child and my child would grow up as best friends and cousins. They would always have each other.

And with the addition of all of our extended families by marriage's kids, we had a huge pack to play with.

"Keeley was up all night as well, according to Addison's parents."

Addison and I had spent the night apart, me at

August's house and her at Paisley's. And while each of us had wanted Keeley with us, Addison's parents wanted to play the best grandparents, the only grandparents if I had anything to say about it, and watch her while we had our night apart. Her parents, as well as my brothers and Paisley would all be taking turns watching Keeley when we were on our honeymoon. Of course, our honeymoon was going to be two parts, a couple of nights alone, and then we were taking Keeley with us. Most people probably didn't want to go on a romantic trip with a baby, but most people weren't us. We wanted Keeley with us. She had been the catapult to bring us together, but I knew we would've ended up together no matter what. There was nothing fake about us, nothing accidental. We were everything, I couldn't wait to prove that to my *wife*, not my girlfriend, not my fiancée, not my best friend. My everything.

"I still think you should change the song."

I flipped August off. "Do you want to talk about your wedding then?"

August scowled at me, and I knew I was a dick for bringing it up, but August was acting like a dick. I also knew why he was, but I wasn't going to harp on it.

"Knock, knock," Ford said from the doorway, and I tilted my head at my brother-in-law. "Is it time?"

"You know it. Noah's out there with the crowd, keeping them entertained, but you guys should get out there. Your bride's waiting."

I didn't even realize I was running until Heath grabbed me by the collar and made me stop.

"*Calmly* make your way down. She's not actually waiting at the other end of the aisle." Heath paused and then we all looked over at Ford. "Is she?"

"No, but she's just as antsy as you are. It's going to be nice to extend the family. I swear there aren't enough of us."

I rolled my eyes, considering how many siblings Ford had and realized that our family was growing by leaps and bounds, and it was about time.

We had spent so long not realizing exactly what our family could be, of course it was time for us to find the family we wanted.

This was it.

This was the damn moment.

I held back a grin—and my breakfast—as we made our way through the doors and into the ceremony.

People smiled and waved, and I tried to do the same.

I wasn't walking in to music. We were keeping this as casual as possible.

When I made it to the front, my brothers with me, everybody took their seats and our officiant nodded at me.

When the music began, my heart raced, and I waited.

Because she was coming to me.

My everything.

Addison's parents walked down the aisle, Keeley in their arms.

Keeley gave me a little wave, one that was all chunky fists and bright smiles, and as everybody made cooing sounds, I held up my arms.

She jumped from Addison's mother's arms right into mine. Everybody gasped, but my brothers threw their heads back and laughed.

I shook my head. "Seriously?" I asked and kissed the top of her head.

"She gets that from your side of the family," Addison's mother said, but I knew she was only kidding.

Of course, Addison had been bungee jumping while I hadn't. So maybe it was a lie.

"You stay with your Grammy and Grandpa, okay?" I asked, and Keeley patted my cheek and kissed my nose. Everybody laughed and somebody sniffled in the crowd as she leapt into her grandfather's arms.

Addison's father was ready for it, and I laughed, knowing that that child was going to give me gray hairs, and I couldn't wait.

Out of the corner of my eye, I realized that two uninvited guests had arrived, but I didn't care.

I felt August stiffen beside me because he had noticed as well, just like Heath.

But we let our parents sit in the back, not making a sound. They didn't touch each other, didn't look at each other. They just looked right at me. I nodded at them in acknowledgment.

I wasn't them. I was never going to be them.

They were the people that tried to ruin us, and they didn't matter anymore.

I was making promises they hadn't kept.

So, fuck them, and fuck what they had done to us.

They weren't ever going to watch their grandchild, because they didn't have one. I wasn't going to let them in her life. Not with the toxicity they brought with them, and because I was pretty sure they would never learn their lessons.

But they weren't part of today. I shook my head at my brothers, making sure we were all set, and the music changed.

Paisley walked down the aisle first, her head high but her eyes unseeing.

I didn't know if it was because she wasn't looking at August, or something else, and I would care soon. But for now, I wanted to focus on the person who would soon be in front of me. The person that I loved.

And I loved her so damn much.

Paisley went to her side, and then Devney, and I heard Heath growl behind me. Well, considering the dress she wore, I understood. Each woman wore a dress that matched them perfectly; Devney in a light-blue mermaid-looking dress, and Paisley had a green flowing dress that made her hair and eyes stand out.

They both looked gorgeous, and I understood.

But the next person to enter was who I was focused on.

The woman coming toward me, face full of joy and radiance, the woman I loved more than anything.

She had on an ivory lace dress that cupped her curves and made her look radiant. Her hair had grown long over the past year thanks to the pregnancy and the fact that she didn't have to have a haircut to make her look fierce and determined. I loved her no matter what she wore or how she did her hair. But she let it flow down her shoulders in long waves that accentuated her beauty.

She walked herself down the aisle, as her parents had walked our child, and as the music turned into *The Lord of the Rings* soundtrack for Arwen, I grinned. We were so fucking geeky and I couldn't help but love it.

Some people cried, but I just stared at the woman who would be my wife and held up my hand.

I loved her with every ounce that I was, and it was finally time.

Time for our next adventure.

She slid her hand into mine and I squeezed it, before we stood up in front of our friends and family, in front of our futures.

And when we said our vows, it was just the beginning.

"You are my best friend and the man I never thought I could love. I knew as soon as I saw you, that you would be in my life. That we would have adventures together and make our friends laugh, and I could always rely on you. I didn't realize that you were part of my heart in more ways than one until it was almost too late. I love you, Luca. I love your compassion, your caring. I love the way you are with animals. I love the way that our house will be forever filled with animals no matter what time of day." People laughed at that, and I smiled, my eyes on her and her alone. "I love that you've given me a daughter that I will cherish for all time. I love you, Luca Cassidy. You are my family. Just like I'm yours. And I can't wait to continue this, forever and always."

She slid the ring on my finger and I squeezed her hand, smiling down at her.

"I love you, Addison. I've loved you for longer than we both care to admit." She laughed at that, and I shook my head, more serious than I'd ever been in my life. "I didn't realize what I wanted in a family, what I could lose. I thought I had lost it before, but you and Keeley are my future. Whatever family we bring together, we are it. I cannot wait to share my life with you, and to bring home those animals I know you love just as much as me." She laughed and I grinned. "And I cannot wait for you to realize that you totally settled when it comes to this relationship."

Everybody laughed as she rolled her eyes. "Really?"

"I'm sorry, I might be a catch, but have you looked at yourself?"

"Hell," August growled from beside us and Heath shushed him.

"I can't wait to see the world with you, and to watch you take over the world. You are fierce, fiery, and you are going to show our daughter that we can be all of that. I cannot wait.

"I love you," I whispered, just for her, and she smiled at me.

"I love you more."

"Agree to disagree," I teased, and when we were pronounced man and wife, I leaned down to kiss my bride, and laughed as our daughter called for both of us.

I held up my arms, and then Keeley was in them, and the three of us were laughing, holding each other, and this was only our beginning.

The beginning of everything.

When our wedding song started, I did my best not to look over at August, who laughed at me, and we danced to Ed Sheeran, and then held Keeley between us as we danced again to another song. And then we did indeed drop it low, and I completely embarrassed myself and did not care. We cut cake, gently fed it to each other because smashing cake into each other's faces meant that I would get kicked in the balls. I knew the rules. And we danced and we ate and we drank and we began our lives together.

"I'm so glad that you were my fake boyfriend."

I laughed as I held her close, a song playing that I knew all the words to, even if I could barely hear it over my heart racing. This was my wife. My wife.

I was so damn lucky.

"We skipped over boyfriend and went directly to fiancé, thank you very much."

She rolled her eyes and laughed at me.

"Yes, I suppose that's true."

"I'm just saying, you fake proposed first."

"You've got me there. I guess the whole fake thing's going to take a little bit to get used to."

"There's nothing fake about us. I love you."

"I love you too. Now, are you going to ravish me in a coat closet like you threatened that one time?"

I groaned, my cock pressing against her stomach. "You do realize that everybody is looking at us? There's no way we can get away."

"I'm pretty sure I can find a way."

She went to her tiptoes and kissed me softly, and ten minutes later we found a way to get away.

And somehow we weren't caught. Thankfully, there was nothing fake about my wife, our coat closet time, or the fact that I couldn't wait to do it again.

NEXT IN THE FIRST TIME SERIES:
Things are going to get messy in Second
Chance Husband with Paisley and August.
I can't wait.

A Note from Carrie Ann Ryan

Thank you so much for reading **Last Minute Fiancé.**

These two characters were so much fun to write. I LOVED their dynamic and how they sort of just fell into a relationship. Considering that's how I ended up marrying my late husband, I couldn't help but smile.

These two also went through so much and I'm happy that they are getting their HEA and can FINALLY rest.

But they aren't the only ones who need to rest. Paisley and August have been fighting me since I first thought of their book and now it's nearly time for their story.

I just don't think any of us are ready for Second Chance Husband...

And if you'd like to read about Greer's story with her two men, you can read it in Best Friend Temptation!

The First Time Series:
Book 1: Good Time Boyfriend
Book 2: Last Minute Fiancé
Book 3: Second Chance Husband

NEXT IN THE FIRST TIME SERIES:
Things are going to get messy in Second Chance Husband with Paisley and August. I can't wait.

IF YOU'D LIKE TO READ A BONUS SCENE: CHECK OUT THIS SPECIAL EPILOGUE!

If you want to make sure you know what's coming next from me, you can sign up for my newsletter at www. CarrieAnnRyan.com; follow me on twitter at @CarrieAnnRyan, or like my Facebook page. I also have a Facebook Fan Club where we have trivia, chats, and other goodies. You guys are the reason I get to do what I do and I thank you.

Make sure you're signed up for my MAILING LIST so

you can know when the next releases are available as well as find giveaways and FREE READS.

Happy Reading!

Also from Carrie Ann Ryan

The Montgomery Ink Legacy Series:

Book 1: Bittersweet Promises (Leif & Brooke)

Book 2: At First Meet (Nick & Lake)

Book 2.5: Happily Ever Never (May & Leo)

Book 3: Longtime Crush (Sebastian & Raven)

Book 4: Best Friend Temptation (Noah, Ford, and Greer)

Book 4.5: Happily Ever Maybe (Jennifer & Gus)

Book 5: Last First Kiss (Daisy & Hugh)

Book 6: His Second Chance (Kane & Phoebe)

Book 7: One Night with You (Kingston & Claire)

The Wilder Brothers Series:

Book 1: One Way Back to Me (Eli & Alexis)

Book 2: Always the One for Me (Evan & Kendall)

Book 3: The Path to You (Everett & Bethany)

Book 4: Coming Home for Us (Elijah & Maddie)

Book 5: Stay Here With Me (East & Lark)

Book 6: Finding the Road to Us (Elliot, Trace, and Sidney)

Book 7: Moments for You (Ridge & Aurora)

Book 7.5: A Wilder Wedding (Amos & Naomi)

Book 8: Forever For Us (Wyatt & Ava)

The First Time Series:

Book 1: Good Time Boyfriend (Heath & Denver)

Book 2: Last Minute Fiancé (Luca & Addison)

Book 3: Second Chance Husband (August & Paisley)

The Montgomery Ink: Fort Collins Series:

Book 1: Inked Persuasion (Jacob & Annabelle)

Book 2: Inked Obsession (Beckett & Eliza)

Book 3: Inked Devotion (Benjamin & Brenna)

Book 3.5: Nothing But Ink (Clay & Riggs)

Book 4: Inked Craving (Lee & Paige)

Book 5: Inked Temptation (Archer & Killian)

The Montgomery Ink: Boulder Series:

Book 1: Wrapped in Ink (Liam & Arden)

Book 2: Sated in Ink (Ethan, Lincoln, and Holland)

Book 3: Embraced in Ink (Bristol & Marcus)

Book 3: Moments in Ink (Zia & Meredith)

Book 4: Seduced in Ink (Aaron & Madison)

Book 4.5: Captured in Ink (Julia, Ronin, & Kincaid)

Book 4.7: Inked Fantasy (Secret ??)

Book 4.8: A Very Montgomery Christmas (The Entire Boulder Family)

Montgomery Ink: Colorado Springs

Book 1: Fallen Ink (Adrienne & Mace)

Book 2: Restless Ink (Thea & Dimitri)

Book 2.5: Ashes to Ink (Abby & Ryan)

Book 3: Jagged Ink (Roxie & Carter)

Book 3.5: Ink by Numbers (Landon & Kaylee)

Montgomery Ink Denver:

Book 0.5: Ink Inspired (Shep & Shea)

Book 0.6: Ink Reunited (Sassy, Rare, and Ian)

Book 1: Delicate Ink (Austin & Sierra)

Book 1.5: Forever Ink (Callie & Morgan)

Book 2: Tempting Boundaries (Decker and Miranda)

Book 3: Harder than Words (Meghan & Luc)

Book 3.5: Finally Found You (Mason & Presley)

Book 4: Written in Ink (Griffin & Autumn)

Book 4.5: Hidden Ink (Hailey & Sloane)

The Less Than Series:

Book 1: Breathless With Her (Devin & Erin)

Book 2: Reckless With You (Tucker & Amelia)

Book 3: Shameless With Him (Caleb & Zoey)

The Fractured Connections Series:

Book 1: Breaking Without You (Cameron & Violet)

Book 2: Shouldn't Have You (Brendon & Harmony)

Book 3: Falling With You (Aiden & Sienna)

Book 4: Taken With You (Beckham & Meadow)

The Whiskey and Lies Series:

Book 1: <u>Whiskey Secrets</u> (Dare & Kenzie)

Book 2: <u>Whiskey Reveals</u> (Fox & Melody)

Book 3: <u>Whiskey Undone</u> (Loch & Ainsley)

The Gallagher Brothers Series:

Book 1: <u>Love Restored</u> (Graham & Blake)

Book 2: <u>Passion Restored</u> (Owen & Liz)

Book 3: <u>Hope Restored</u> (Murphy & Tessa)

The Ravenwood Coven Series:

Book 1: Dawn Unearthed

Book 2: Dusk Unveiled

Book 3: Evernight Unleashed

Book 4.5: <u>Blurred Expectations</u>
Book 4.7: <u>Forgiveness</u>
Book 5: <u>Shattered Emotions</u>
Book 6: <u>Hidden Destiny</u>
Book 6.5: <u>A Beta's Haven</u>
Book 7: <u>Fighting Fate</u>
Book 7.5: <u>Loving the Omega</u>
Book 7.7: <u>The Hunted Heart</u>
Book 8: <u>Wicked Wolf</u>

The Elements of Five Series:
Book 1: From Breath and Ruin
Book 2: From Flame and Ash
Book 3: From Spirit and Binding
Book 4: From Shadow and Silence

Dante's Circle Series:
Book 1: <u>Dust of My Wings</u>
Book 2: <u>Her Warriors' Three Wishes</u>
Book 3: <u>An Unlucky Moon</u>
Book 3.5: <u>His Choice</u>
Book 4: <u>Tangled Innocence</u>
Book 5: <u>Fierce Enchantment</u>
Book 6: <u>An Immortal's Song</u>
Book 7: <u>Prowled Darkness</u>
Book 8: Dante's Circle Reborn

About the Author

Carrie Ann Ryan is the New York Times and USA Today bestselling author of contemporary, paranormal, and young adult romance. Her works include the Montgomery Ink, Redwood Pack, Fractured Connections, and Elements of Five series, which have sold over 3.0 million books worldwide. She started writing while in graduate school for her advanced degree in chemistry and hasn't stopped since. Carrie Ann has written over seventy-five novels and novellas with more in the works. When she's not losing herself in her emotional and action-packed worlds, she's reading as much as she can while wrangling her clowder of cats who have more followers than she does.

www.CarrieAnnRyan.com